AINSLEY KEATON

The Malibu Girls

VINCI

BOOKS

By Ainsley Keaton

Sconset Beach

Vinci Books

vinci-books.com

Published by Vinci Books Ltd in 2025

1

Copyright © Ainsley Keaton 2022

The publisher and the author have made every effort to obtain permissions for any third party material used in this book and to comply with copyright law. Any queries in this respect should be brought to the attention of the publisher and any omissions will be corrected in future editions.

A CIP catalogue record for this book is available from the British Library.

Paperback ISBN: 9781036703769

Chapter One

Ava

Ava arrived back at Nantucket, determined to try to do something about the house she'd inherited. She'd talked to Sarah at length about the possibility of moving back to California, and she was starting to get excited about the prospect.

Like Sarah, Ava was bored for much of the year in Nantucket. The pace was just too slow, and her business, such as it was, relied upon tourists, which were only prominent for three months out of the year. Everything was hopping from Memorial Day to Labor Day - the bars, the restaurants, the nightlife, the country clubs - everything was going all the time. Her bed and breakfast was always full during the summer months. But after Labor Day, everything quieted down, and everything was so slow that Ava often found herself without something to do. And, for somebody who was used to the fast pace of a large law firm in New York City, boredom was deadly.

When she first moved to Nantucket, it was a welcome respite. Her life in New York City was extremely stressful - she hated working for her law firm because it relied upon shady wealthy people trying to get out of paying their taxes, which appalled Ava. She'd spent so many years working 70 hours a week, so, at first, Nantucket was like an extended vacation. But the town had long since lost its appeal, although she had her best friends and sister there, which made life on the island bearable and sometimes exciting. But now Sarah was going to move to California, along with Quinn, and Ava couldn't think of anything less appealing than staying on the island without two of her anchors.

There were two things she was going to try to do - one, she was going to see what she could do about selling her home there on Nantucket. The terms of the will dictated that she couldn't sell the house for five years, and she'd only been in the house for two. Not even that. So, obviously, if she wanted to sell the house, she was in danger of losing it.

The second thing she wanted to do immediately was to talk to Hallie and see what she thought about the possibility of moving out to California. After all, Hallie was only on Nantucket because Ava and Quinn had moved out there. If Ava and Quinn left the island, along with Sarah, then Hallie wouldn't know anybody on the island aside from Willow.

So, the first thing Ava decided to do was talk to an attorney. Quinn had recommended a woman by the name of Estrella Benton, who was a friend of Quinn's friend, Asher. Asher was somebody Quinn had been tempted to date on several occasions but had decided against it. Things were just not quite right. But Asher was a good friend to Quinn, so she was always in contact with him, and he gave Estrella's name. Estrella lived in Boston, so that's where Ava was headed on the Monday after she got back to Nantucket.

She arrived at Estrella's office, located in a high rise in the heart of Boston. Estrella's office was on the 50th floor, which boded well, in Ava's opinion, because it meant Estrella was probably a successful attorney. The only people who could afford an office on such a high floor were people who did very well in their profession.

Estrella herself came out to greet Ava when Ava got to the office. "Hello, Ava," she said. "Come on in."

Ava followed Estrella to her office, which was all hardwood floors, gleaming corner desks, and eclectic artwork on the wall. Estrella was a bit of an imposing figure, as she was almost 6 feet tall, with long braided hair and beautiful cocoa au lait skin. She spoke with an accent that Ava pinpointed as South African.

Estrella smiled. "How can I help you?"

Ava explained what she was trying to do. She told Estrella all about the will, how she apparently was stuck with the house for the next three years, and how she wanted to sell the house so she could buy something in Malibu.

Estrella nodded her head. "Let me ask you a question. In this case, if you sold the house or otherwise violated the terms of the will conditions, does the document specify who would get the house if you violated the conditions?"

Ava shook her head. "No, it doesn't specify. No alternate heir is named if the will fails because I violated its conditions."

"Well then, the laws of succession would come into play here. Is there a surviving spouse?" the beautiful attorney asked.

Ava thought about Esther, James' wife, and a chill went up her spine. She didn't want to do one thing in the world, and that was to confront Esther about any of this. Ava assumed Esther didn't know about her, even though Morty,

James' best friend from way back, told Ava that her birth was a way of saving their marriage because Esther also had a child out of wedlock.

The situation was that James, the man who willed her the house on Nantucket, had an affair with her mother back in the 1960s when he was married to Esther. Ava was a result of that affair. Ava found this out recently when her mother came clean, and that caused a huge rift between them for a bit. Ava had long since forgiven her mother, but she never wanted to confront James' family.

Esther was still alive. She was in her early 90s, and Ava didn't know much about her other than that she was quite elderly. Ava didn't want to talk to her. She was still ashamed of everything that happened and how her birth came about, even though she didn't need to be. It wasn't her fault. Her mother was the one who had an affair, not her, yet she felt guilty for it all.

Ava nodded her head. "Yes, there is a surviving spouse."

"OK. Are you friendly with the surviving spouse?"

"No. In fact, I've never talked to her. It's very complicated."

"You should probably contact her if you want to do something with the will. There's no way you can avoid the will's terms. What James Bloch did here was a 'Dead Hand' clause. He's trying to control the disposal of his house from beyond the grave. Sometimes these 'Dead Hand' clauses can be void if they're against public policy. An example of this would be a clause where the will is valid only if the benefactor divorces her husband. That would be against public policy because it isn't a good thing to demand a divorce, so that would be one way of getting out of that particular clause. But in your case, there's nothing like that. So the clause is the clause. The only thing you could do is talk to the surviving spouse and see if she could deed the house over to you once she receives it."

Ava felt hopeful that there was a way of disposing of the house. She knew that if she sold the Nantucket house, she could buy a nice house in Malibu. Yet, she wasn't too encouraged about what she had to do to get out from under the terms of the will.

"Tell me how all this will work."

"I'll give a call to the executor of the estate and explain what's happening. Once you sell the house or take a lien against it, the will becomes void and the surviving heir automatically gets the property. And then she could sign the deed to you, so you have the house free and clear. That would be the best approach if you can get her to agree to do that. In fact, that would be the only way you could get out from under the terms of the will."

Ava thought about this approach. She knew one way she could violate the will's terms: ask her mother to take a lien against the house. Ava didn't believe she could actually get a mortgage against the house because any mortgage holder would do a record check, find out the terms of the will, and refuse to give Ava a mortgage. But her mother would do it if she asked her to.

All of this seemed extremely risky, however. She could talk to Esther and ask her if she'd be willing to participate in this transaction. Ava felt she had nothing to lose if she asked her. If she said no, then that was that. Ava would stay in the house or hire somebody to run the place full-time. Jessica, the young lady who had been staying with her in exchange for working around the inn, was also going to move to Los Angeles because Andrew, the musician she was in love with, was moving out to the West Coast to be closer to his recording studios.

So it'd be a matter of Ava finding somebody to run the inn, but that wouldn't be easy. Unfortunately, because the island was so quiet for most of the year, it'd be difficult to find somebody to stay there full-time throughout the year.

After talking with Sarah about the possibility of moving out to California, Ava became excited. But, she was becoming less excited now because it looked like she would have to go ahead and stay in the house after all.

But she wasn't going to go down without a fight. She drew a breath as she thought about the possibility of having to talk to Esther face to face. She would have to meet the woman who was married to Ava's father when Ava was born. The woman who was betrayed by James. She didn't want to open that wound.

But, then again, there was a reasonable assumption that Esther knew all about her. Morty told Ava that since Esther also had a baby out of wedlock, the two mistakes essentially canceled one another out. Because of this, Esther and James could move forward in their marriage. So, the assumption was that Esther knew all about Ava.

She would definitely have to talk to Sarah about what she should do.

Ava thanked Estrella for the advice, paid her, and left.

That evening, Ava hosted Sarah, Quinn, and Hallie at her house. She ordered organic food from an organic restaurant on the island and, of course, had a bottle of wine ready to go. The ladies always liked to get together when they had a pressing need, and today was no exception.

In fact, because of everything that was happening, there was more need than ever for the ladies to come together.

Ava hoped she wasn't making the wrong decision, but she was afraid that she was.

"So, here's the deal," Ava told the ladies. "I need to talk to Esther, James' surviving spouse. I need to ask her if she'd be willing to participate in a transaction where I do something to void the will. She would get the house automatically when I take this action, and then she would just deed me the house once she took possession of it. It's very risky. Because what if she lies to me and says she's going to do it but then doesn't? That would be the worst-case scenario. I mean, if she just said 'no,' my path is set. I'll have to stay here."

It wouldn't be the worst thing in the world, having to stay in this beautiful house on Nantucket. Still, without Quinn and Sarah on the island with her, it would be an empty existence. Ava never appreciated how much she relied upon her posse to keep her spirits up daily. Now, she was faced with two of her anchors moving across the country. The thought made her want to vomit.

It was really true that people need people. And it's not always easy to find your person in life. Ava had yet to find her person in the form of a romantic relationship, but she definitely found her person, or people, with Hallie, Quinn, and Sarah. They were a unit. They were the village for her. If they were going to move to California, then Ava was too.

Besides, she was bored.

So bored.

Sarah understood why Ava was very hesitant to talk to Esther. "Ava, I know what you're getting at. You don't want to talk to Esther because you don't want to drive a stake through her heart. But, then again, you told me Esther knew James had an affair and a child out of wedlock. And she probably knew that that child was you. So, I don't think you have much to worry about. I'm sure she already knows about you, and, for all you know, she'll welcome you with open arms."

"But what if she doesn't? What if she slams the door in my face?" Ava knew the answer to that question before she even asked it. If Esther slammed the door in her face, then she slammed the door in her face. There was nothing that could be done at that point.

"It's worth a shot," Sarah said. "Ava, I'm looking forward to moving to California because I believe that's where I belong. But I'm not looking forward to leaving you behind. I mean, it seems like we've been making up for lost time. I feel closer to you now than I ever have. Things just won't be quite right if you're not out there with me. So, I think you should go ahead and at least try it."

Quinn smiled. "Goes without saying, I agree. I already had my eye on a house out there. I'm thinking about moving to the Venice Beach area. They have such beautiful turn-of-the-century homes, some of them facing canals. I'd be dying to get ahold of one of those older homes and work my magic."

Quinn was referring to some of the big old houses in the Venice Beach area built by a developer named Abbot Kinney in 1905. Kinney wanted to recreate the feel and vibe of Venice, Italy, so he built the canals and the homes that faced these canals. There were quite a few of those old homes because the Venice Beach area seemed to be an older area of town. Ava had visited the Venice Beach area because, when she was with Sarah visiting Mary, the sister of Sarah's now-deceased boyfriend Max, Ava explored the city while Sarah was gone. Mary lived in Malibu, so she and Sarah stayed at a Malibu resort.

The Venice Beach area wasn't far away from the Malibu

area, only about a 10-minute drive, and she went there one evening to catch the vibe and see how things were out there.

It seemed to be a very lively area of town. On the beach was a spinning class of about 50 people with glowing headphones. On the grassy area, around 100 young people with glowing sticks were having a dance party. There were bars and restaurants right on the beach and they all seemed to be hopping. And, because it was California, Ava thought the nightlife on Venice Beach was probably hopping all year round, unlike here on Nantucket. And all through the beach were little enclaves with chairs and people hanging around. It seemed like a fun, lively atmosphere, and Ava thought it'd be a nice place for Quinn to settle with her young daughter.

Just down the street from the beach was the Santa Monica pier, another lively place to go. The Santa Monica pier was like a mini carnival, with musicians, magicians, face painters, artists, and seafood restaurants up and down the pier. The Santa Monica pier was a place where people liked to gather in the evenings, as the sunset behind the Santa Monica hills provided the backdrop to Santa Monica and Malibu.

Ava thought living in the Venice Beach or Santa Monica areas would be a good idea. But she also loved the homes that were part of the Malibu Lagoon State Beach. She went hiking along the little trail there, admiring the beautiful sycamore, pine and pepper trees that grew wild around the lagoon, and she was more than impressed with the homes that were right on the beach. These homes were, like the Venice Beach area, older, although they didn't seem as old as the Venice Beach houses. Most of them were probably built around the 1940s or 1950s, and they sported huge decks that jetted out of the homes. The water came all the way up to the retaining walls that all the homes had to keep the surf away from their buildings.

Ava thought if she lived in Malibu, it would be the best of both worlds - she could still sit on her deck and listen to the waves rolling in every night. And that was something she'd gotten used to there on Nantucket. Her favorite time of the day was when she could sit on her deck, close her eyes and hear the surf coming in. She'd miss that if she didn't have it.

However, with the Malibu Lagoon State Beach homes, she'd still be able to hear the surf rolling in from her window or deck, and she could just relax. At the same time, it was close enough to the liveliness of the Santa Monica Pier and the Venice Beach areas that she could enjoy the liveliness and nightlife of those areas when she felt like it.

"Quinn, I agree that the beautiful older homes on Venice Beach would be perfect for you. With your interior decorating eye, you could make one of those houses shine like a diamond."

Ava would have also loved to get a house on Venice Beach, but she couldn't find one that was right on the beach like they had in Malibu. That was the only reason why Malibu was a much more attractive prospect for her than the Venice Beach area.

Sarah took a deep breath. "I'm really looking forward to moving out to California, too. It's a bit of a shame because I just bought the house here. But, I already have a few offers to buy my house for $2.5 million, which is much more than what I paid. So I'll be able to get a nice little bungalow out in California. I won't be able to afford anything as nice as what you're going to get, Ava, assuming you can get out from under your house here. But I think I can find a home in the Venice Beach area that would be in my price range.

And I'm looking forward to maybe finding a job at a winery. They have quite a few up in the Santa Monica hills. I visited them while I was out there."

Ava had also visited the wineries in the Santa Monica hills. Ava had to admit it was a bit scary that a winery was high in those hills. To get to the winery, she had to drive up a lot of very windy roads that went straight up a mountain. Many of those roads didn't even have the semblance of a guardrail. And, to make things even more dangerous, people tended to tailgate drivers out there. Ava thought that wine tasting and driving down those hills didn't go hand in hand. She shuddered to think about driving drunk, misjudging a curve and sailing down the ravine.

Yet, she thought the winery she'd visited was a beautiful one. It was a very hot day when they went there, unseasonably warm, considering it was only April. She had a glass of wine while looking over the panoramic views afforded by being so high in the hills. The winery had all different kinds of cabernets and merlots and chablis. Ava drank a bit too much, and since she was driving, she had to hang out there for several hours until she sobered up. It was a beautiful evening, and Ava thought this winery would be a perfect place for Sarah to land.

Sarah and Ava had even talked about the possibility of buying their own winery. That was actually the goal.

Ava wasn't clear about what she would do once she got to Malibu. She had experience running a bed and breakfast, and she had experience as a lawyer. However, she'd long since decided that law was not for her. So she and Sarah had fantasized one night while they were in California about buying a winery in the Santa Monica hills. That was something Ava could possibly do if she made enough money off the sale of her Nantucket house. They could even get their mother to get in on the deal. Their mother was still a judge in Boston, but she was always looking for investment opportunities. She originally had invested in Ava's bed and breakfast on Nantucket. In fact, without her investment, Ava probably wouldn't have been able to have opened up. Or, at least, she wouldn't have been able to have the luxury she had there on Nantucket. So, her mother helped her. However, once Ava and her mother, Colleen, made up and decided they'd have a true mother and daughter relationship from that point on, Colleen told Ava she didn't want any of the profits from her bed and breakfast. That showed Ava she was ready to move on in their relationship and become closer.

But, if Ava and Sarah were going to ask Colleen to invest in the winery, they'd make sure it was much more of a business relationship. They imagined Colleen would be a silent partner in this endeavor.

Of course, at the moment, this was all pipe dreams. But it was something Ava was allowing herself to dream about. She'd absolutely love to be in business with her sister. And she wanted more than anything for Sarah to have a substantial position. At the moment, Sarah was just working for Ava as a sommelier. Sarah was perfectly happy doing that, but Ava knew Sarah could be so much more. She could do so much more with her life. And owning a winery would be something that could really challenge Sarah and make her happy. Ava wanted that for her sister.

Of course, all of this turned to whether Ava could sell her home there on Nantucket.

Hallie was quiet for a little bit. Ava knew Hallie would end up coming out to California with them, but she was a little hesitant about what she would do when she got out there. She was trying to make a name for herself in the life coaching realm. She had a few clients there on Nantucket. One of them was an artist by the name of Conrad, who was very prominent, and Hallie had a thing for him. Hallie also helped Ava's daughter, Charlotte, when Charlotte was trying to figure out her life. Hallie had battled breast cancer, but the last time she went for a checkup, she was informed she was cancer free.

"What's going on, Hallie?" Ava asked her. "What are you thinking?"

Hallie started to laugh. "Well, it turns out that Morgan, her wife, Emma Claire, and their new adopted child, Zendaya, are moving to Los Angeles. The art gallery business in San Francisco is a little on the wane. I guess many of the San Francisco artists are moving down to Los Angeles because that's where the new art scene is. Morgan and Emma Claire are going to buy a home in Los Angeles and raise their child there. But I don't want her thinking I'm following her again."

That was one thing that Hallie always worried about. When Morgan was young, Hallie latched on to her and tried to make Morgan's life her own. That was because, at that time, Hallie didn't really have a life to speak of. She was married to a very toxic man and wasn't working outside the home. So, when Morgan started to branch out a little, working at an art gallery as a curator, Hallie tried to ride her coattails. Hallie volunteered for a job at the same art gallery. She made a pest of herself, so much so that the gallery owner told her not to come around anymore. And then, when Morgan moved across the country to San Francisco, Hallie felt it was because she was overbearing.

But things were very good between Hallie and Morgan these days. And part of the reason why was because they lived across the country from one another. Morgan came to visit Hallie from time to time, and Hallie did the same for Morgan. Hallie worried that the same toxic codependency relationship would emerge again if they lived in the same city.

Ava put her arm around Hallie. "Hallie, don't worry about it. You're a different person than you were when she was growing up. You're no longer in that same relationship with your husband. You're making a life for yourself. You're working on getting your nutrition counseling license. You're becoming a life coach. You're not the same woman who didn't know who she was and where she was going. So you're not going to be the same person who smothers Morgan."

"I know what you're saying, but I'm afraid Morgan will think I'm out there because of her. She just moved out there. She just opened up a new gallery out there." Hallie shook her head. "The last thing I want to happen is I start smothering her without even thinking about it, and she pulls away from me. I mean, it's going to be good to be in the same city as her, don't get me wrong. I just have to watch myself and ensure I don't make her feel like I'm hovering."

To be honest, Ava worried about the same thing with Jackson. Jackson was her son and an actor in Los Angeles who just got a major part in a major movie opposite the biggest A-list actress in the world, Emma Ross. Ava worried about Jackson constantly. Before he got this part, she worried he wouldn't make it in Hollywood. He was doing quite well with the modeling business. Acting, not so much. And, now that he got this major part in this major movie, Ava worried he wouldn't do well. Maybe the movie wouldn't do well, or critics would savage him, and he would never make another movie again. That happened to quite a few people over the years. They were unknown, they had a big movie, the movie flopped, and they were never heard from again. It was so much pressure on her son, Ava just couldn't stand it. So Ava worried that she, too, would smother her son.

"Sugar, you're going to be fine," Quinn said to Hallie. "Things are going very well for you and Morgan. And, you have your best friends around you. We'll make sure that you don't go overboard with her."

The ladies listened to the surf and drank their wine. It was a beautiful evening in April. The island would start gearing up again in a few more weeks for the summer rush. Ava's inn would be filled to the brim with people and a waiting list.

But Ava hoped that by the end of the month, she would be selling her house and heading out to California.

Chapter Two

Ava

Ava had nervously made an appointment to see Esther Bloch. The older lady was still living in New York City. Brooklyn, to be exact.

When Ava called Esther, she was amazed that Esther knew exactly who she was and, in fact, was eager to speak with her. So, that was a huge relief for Ava. She imagined that Esther would slam the phone down on her when she called her. And, if Esther slammed the phone down on her, Ava would figure she deserved it.

Instead, Esther spoke warmly on the phone. "Sure, I'll meet with you. To tell you the truth, I've always been curious about you. I've never had the guts to actually call you myself. I figured that you probably didn't want to talk to me. And, I also had it in my head that maybe you didn't know the truth about your father. But I guess you do know the truth about my James. So, sure, I'd love to meet you."

So Ava found herself flying into New York City and

heading across the bridge to Brooklyn. Her heart was in her throat after she called her Uber and found herself heading toward Esther's home. Yes, Esther was extremely friendly with her on the phone. But meeting her face to face would be a completely different story. And she also was going to find out more about her half-siblings. There were two other daughters - Rachel and Deborah - along with a son who had a different father from James. That son's name was Elijah, and he was the only one in the Bloch family with no blood relation to Ava. Elijah was about Ava's age.

There also was another daughter who was murdered - Valerie. She was Jessica's mother.

Ava found that she was actually looking forward to possibly meeting Rachel, Deborah, and even Elijah. Rachel and Deborah had the same father as Ava, so they were her half-sisters. Ava was looking forward to learning more about that part of her family tree.

Ava got to Esther's home and knocked on the door. It was a beautiful brownstone with bay windows and was built probably around 1900 or so. The neighborhood was quiet and treelined, the kind of neighborhood that Ava always loved to visit during the autumn months because the spectacular foliage gave these streets a kind of glow. Like a typical Brooklyn neighborhood, the brownstones were interspersed with coffee shops, delis, restaurants, and a bar here and there.

After she knocked on the door, a man answered it. Ava deduced the guy was the butler by his demeanor.

"Hello," he said in a very formal manner. "You must be Ava Flynn. Esther is waiting for you in the parlor."

The man led Ava back through the house to a room in the back that must have been the parlor. The brownstone was beautiful - high ceilings, chandeliers, hardwood floors, and the beautiful old crown molding that Ava always admired in these older homes. The brownstone was fronted by an enormous bay window with three panels and a cushion.

Ava arrived at the parlor and saw a tiny woman sitting in a high-backed chair next to the fireplace. She was wearing glasses that she lowered to the end of her nose to get a closer look at Ava.

She nodded her head and then stood up. "Ava Flynn. At long last, we meet."

She extended her hand, and Ava shook it. As she shook Esther's hand, she looked at her own hand and saw it was shaking like a leaf. "I'm so sorry. I'm just really nervous about meeting you."

At that, Esther started to laugh heartily. "Goodness. I've always felt the same way about you. I've known about you since the beginning, you know."

Ava's nodded. "That's what I understand," she said.

Esther shook her head. "That was a really bad time in our marriage. I know you've met with Morty, so I know you know the broad contours about what happened. I was caring for my sick mother here in New York, and I met a man while I was here in New York City. His name was Michael Steiner. We had a brief fling, and I had a child with him. And around the same time, James was having an affair with your mother, and he fathered you with her. We weren't speaking at that time, James and me. When I met Michael, I fell head over heels in love with him. I didn't even think about James in Cambridge, who was waiting for me to come home. But then, after I got pregnant with Elijah, I realized I didn't want to be with Michael. I realized my husband, James, was who I belonged with. He was who I took vows with. My mother passed away while I was caring for her, and after that, I returned to James."

Ava quietly listened to her. It seemed that Esther wanted to unburden herself about what happened during that time.

"And you were pregnant with Elijah when you returned to him?"

"Yes. And I had to tell him about it. It was the hardest thing I've ever done, looking the man I love in the eye and telling him I was pregnant with another man's child. And he reacted to my story very calmly. It turns out he had the same secret he was afraid to tell me about - he had fathered a child with your mother, Colleen."

Esther looked out the window, her rheumy blue eyes getting misty. Ava instinctively wanted to hug the woman, but she didn't really know her, so she put her hand on hers.

Esther finally just shook her head. "What a mess we got ourselves into. But we decided we were going to go and see a marital counselor. There was so much hurt between us. So much pain, so much rage that was coursing through our marriage. We had so many hurtful words that we had said to one another that just couldn't be taken back. But the marital counselor was able to put us on a good footing. And I know if I'd returned to James pregnant with another man's child, he would've rightfully told me to turn around and leave the house if he didn't make the same mistake himself. Because he made the same mistake I did, having an affair, thinking that affair was going to somehow fix the hole inside both of our souls, we could go forward and forgive one another. It was so difficult. It was years of counseling. Twice a week counseling. But we were able to rebuild our marriage, brick by brick, day by day, second by second. And, about five years after Elijah and you were born, we turned a corner. We fell back in love. We felt like we did when we first got married."

Her eyes were now getting misty, and she shook her head. Ava's heart went out to her, for it was obvious that Esther really missed her James, the love of her life and her husband for over 65 years.

"I always was grateful for you," Esther said. "Because of your birth, I was able to have 65 years with the man I loved. And if you were never born, I probably would've been divorced from my James in 1968 or somewhere around there. I would've never gotten those extra 50-odd years with my James."

Esther looked at the needlepoint she was working on when Ava first entered the parlor. Her hands were that of a woman over 90 - wrinkled, with fine skin, brown spots and blue veins showing through. Her blue eyes were cloudy. Yet, she had the posture of a much younger woman. She sat perfectly straight in her chair. She was a proud woman, Ava could tell. And how humiliating it must've been for her to admit to James about Elijah.

"Esther, thank you for telling me this story. I know I got some of the story from Morty like you say. But it really means a lot to hear it from you. And I'm so sorry all this happened to you and James."

Esther shook her head. "Dear, please don't say that. Elijah has been a light in my life. He's such a good man. He's a doctor. He's saved countless lives in Africa when he worked with Doctors Without Borders. I couldn't imagine what the world would be like without him. So, I can never regret having him. I could never regret the affair I had with his father. Because without that affair, there would be no Elijah. And without Elijah, all the people he saved might not have been. It's like that movie, *It's a Wonderful Life*. In that movie, George Bailey's life touched so many other lives. Without his birth, his brother would have died, and the druggist would have been in prison. And his brother saved a lot of people himself. It's just like the butterfly theory. That butterfly floats his wings, and the repercussions go on forever. In this case, the repercussions were amazing. No, the world is a much better place because Elijah is in it."

Ava wondered if Esther thought about having a pregnancy termination when she discovered she was pregnant with Elijah. Ava thought that was probably what she would've done. If she got pregnant with another man's child while she was married and she thought that the birth would be the end of the marriage, she probably would've gotten an abortion to keep the pregnancy secret from her husband.

Of course, Ava was never going to ask Esther that question. But Esther seemed to know what she was thinking.

"I thought about it, you know. Terminating. Of course, back then, it wasn't so easy to do. Abortion wasn't legal everywhere. It wasn't legal in New York at that time. New York didn't legalize it until 1970. Even in Massachusetts, abortion was only legal when the mother's life was threatened. Of course, I was a woman of means. I was married to the son of a very wealthy man. I could have gone overseas to have it done. But, then again, that would involve my telling James, which defeated the purpose of getting an abortion. But, believe me, I prayed about it every night. I was so afraid that he would tell me the marriage was over when I told him the truth about Elijah. But I'm so glad I had the courage to tell him. And we had the courage to move forward."

Esther had a smile on her face that made Ava feel very warm inside. This older lady had so much love in her heart, that was obvious. And she seemed to even have a love for

Ava. She'd just met Ava, but then again, she knew about her for all these years. So, maybe she had developed an affection for the idea of Ava long ago.

"I'm very happy for you and James," Ava said. "It's wonderful to find a great love. And it's even better to really fight for that love." Ava thought about Daniel, the love of her life. What she wouldn't give for the opportunity to have fought for him. But he died in a car accident right before the birth of the triplets. She also thought about Christopher, the husband who cleaned out her bank account. Christopher tried to come back to her, but Ava wasn't having it. Ironically, Christopher fathered a child with another woman while he was married to Ava. He actually married that other woman, making him a bigamist. But Ava didn't really care about that, because she had long stopped caring about Christopher as a romantic relationship. So she could take the stunning news that he had a second family at one time in stride.

"Yes, dear," Esther said. "James was the love of my life. I was so foolish when I met Michael Steiner. I was 35 years old, barely a baby, now that I think about it. Of course, when you get to my age, everybody seems like a baby to you. Even you. I look at you right now, and you seem so young to me. But, I was 35, my mother was dying, and I was just in a very bad state when I met Michael. That's all I could think about. I mistook his affection for me for love. And love was what I desperately needed at that time. James was pulling away from me, and with my mother dying, I was so lost."

Ava's heart went out to the older lady. It was clear that, like her own mother, Esther had so many regrets. But one of those regrets was a beautiful thing, Elijah. It was just how things were supposed to be, probably. If Ava believed in the concept of fate, that everything happened for a reason, she thought that was probably the case here. Elijah was meant to be born, and that was that.

Esther finally took a deep breath. "Now, you are here for a reason. I kind of understood that when you called me. I know you probably were curious about me like I've always been curious about you. But I know that you're here for some other reason."

She raised her eyebrows at Ava, and Ava briefly lost her voice.

"Yes," she said to Esther. "Yes, I am here for a reason."

Ava told Esther all about the will and the conditions. "And, since you're the surviving spouse, you're his closest heir. So, if I do something to void my gift, you'll automatically get the property. So, I'd like to do something to violate the will so that you'll get the property. And then, after you get the property, I'd like you to deed it to me. Free and clear."

Esther nodded her head. "Is that all? Dear, when you called me, I knew you wanted something. And, to be honest with you, whatever you were going to ask me, within reason, I would have given to you. I always felt that you got a raw deal, never knowing your actual father. And, it was my idea to put you into James' will. Well, not really. James was going to always put you into his will, but he wasn't going to necessarily give you that house. We talked about it, and I gave him the idea that you might enjoy that house. And it's worth a lot of money. I want you to have it. I didn't want James to put the stipulations in the will that you had to stay in there for five years. I thought that was excessive. But he wanted you to enjoy the house and feared that you'd just sell the house immediately. I think he wanted you to give Nantucket a chance. He always loved it there. That was his favorite place to go, that house. And then he let our granddaughter, Jessica, live there while recovering from her drug addiction. But he always loved that home."

Esther seemed to take a deep breath.

"So, you'll be willing to participate in this transaction?"

"Of course. As I said earlier, I would have lost James if it weren't for your birth. I know that. He would have never forgiven me for having a child with somebody else if he didn't make the same mistake at the same time. So I always thought you were why I spent so many years with the man I loved so much. So, yes, I would be happy to do anything for you."

"And your daughters, Rachel and Deborah? And your son, Elijah? They won't be upset that you're just going to deed the house to me, free and clear?"

"Dear, what if I said the word no. What would you do?"

"I would stay in the house until the five years were up."

"There's your answer. If I turned you down, you would just keep the house. Either way, none of my children would actually get the house. So they don't even have to know about this transaction, to be honest with you. I'll admit that Rachel was slightly upset you got that house. She always loved that house. But she wasn't too upset about it. She lives in a beautiful condo on the Upper West Side, and she's doing very well for herself. And she has a beach house in the Hamptons. So does Deborah. Elijah has a beach house, too, in Malibu."

"So, all your children have beach houses?"

"Yes. My husband had quite a few properties around the country and ensured that all of our children were taken care of. As for me, I'm perfectly happy here in this brownstone. I don't much like the beach. I never did. Too hot, too sandy, and I have very fair skin, so I would get really horrible sunburns. My kids always loved the beach, but I never did. So, I have no desire to have that house on Nantucket, either. Don't worry. You're not going to be stepping on anybody's toes by taking this house free and clear. Just tell me what I need to do, and I will do it."

"OK. Then I'll go ahead and get my lawyer to draw up the paperwork, contact the executor, and explain what's happening. I need to have my mother take out a small lien against the house, which would void the bequest. Once the bequest is voided, it's just a matter of the executor putting the house into your name, and then you would just transfer the deed to me."

Esther started to laugh. "Oh my goodness, so much cloak and dagger. Well, that's OK. I'll be happy if you get the house at the end of all this rigamarole. And you don't have to worry about staying on that tiny island much longer. By the way, where do you plan on moving to?"

"Ironically enough, I'm going to look at beach houses in Malibu. So, maybe when I get out to California, I can give my stepbrother Elijah a call. Do you think he'd mind?"

Ava thought getting to know her stepbrother was a good idea. She was hungry for information about her father, James, and Elijah would be able to supply that for her. And it was so convenient that he happened to be living out in Malibu, where Ava would hopefully get a house now that she could sell her Nantucket house.

"No, dear, I think he'd love to talk to you," Esther said.

Ava spent most of the afternoon talking with Esther. Esther gave her a lot of good insight about her father, James, and Ava was so grateful that she did this. She was not just grateful because, of course, she'd be able to sell her Nantucket home and establish a new life out in California. The thought of moving out there and hopefully opening up a winery with Sarah excited her. And it also excited her that she could enjoy year-round sunshine and warm weather. She was getting very tired of the harsh winters in this north-eastern town, and she had only experienced the winters not even two times. But she'd lived in New York before she came to Nantucket, so harsh winters had been a thing that she had just had to live with. But now, maybe she wouldn't have to. And that excited her very much.

After she left Esther's home and got in her Uber, she smiled.

California, here I come!

Chapter Three

Willow

Willow Killeen was in Los Angeles. She had helped her man, or whatever he was, Jackson, get a major part in a major film based on the life of Zelda Fitzgerald, the wife of F. Scott Fitzgerald, the legendary writer who chronicled the Jazz Age and wrote *The Great Gatsby*, which was considered by some critics to be the greatest novel ever written.

Jackson Flynn, Ava's son, was, unfortunately for Willow, Willow's soul mate. Willow didn't want to be in Los Angeles because she didn't want to be close to him. She was just too independent and never wanted to give her life to a man. Yet, she was compelled to come to Los Angeles and help him.

Willow was compelled to help Jackson by the ghost of Zelda Fitzgerald and the ghost of Clara Bow, who was a 1920s silent star. They both told her she had to help Jackson because he was giving up hope on ever getting a part in Hollywood - he had been out in Hollywood for six years and hadn't gotten a part yet. And so, that's what she did - she helped him get a part in a major film. Along the way, she became compelled to write the screenplay for Zelda because Zelda insisted she do so.

Willow hated being sensitive, which was what she considered herself. She was sometimes in touch with the spirit world, as ghosts occasionally haunted her when they needed her help. Whenever that happened, Willow cursed her "gift," such as it was. That was certainly the case when the two nosy ghosts, Zelda Fitzgerald and Clara Bow, showed up to force Willow to help Jackson out.

Willow had been spending time with Jackson, and she'd spent the night with him the night before. Although she spent the night with Jackson, they didn't go too far. They ended up kissing like teenagers, but that was it. It wasn't going to go further than that, even though she had spent many eons with the man, as he was her soulmate and had been with her through the ages.

When she woke up after spending the night on Jackson's couch, she discovered that Zelda and Clara were both gone.

Jackson had already left his apartment because he had early meetings with the movie director in the Zelda Fitzgerald biopic he would be starring in. When Willow looked around the apartment, she saw that nobody was around.

Willow bit her bottom lip and grimaced. What was going on? She didn't know. All she knew was that she was under contract to ghostwrite a screenplay based on the life of Zelda Fitzgerald, based on the fact that Zelda was haunting Willow and Zelda was going to dictate her story to the young psychic.

Now, Zelda was gone.

Great, just great. Now, what was she supposed to do?

When Zelda was haunting her, it was decided that Zelda would tell her story to Willow, and Willow would write the screenplay based on it. But now that Zelda was gone, Willow wasn't sure what to do.

The first thing she would have to do would be to call Nancy Tallow, the official writer for the Zelda Fitzgerald biopic screenplay. Willow couldn't assume that the ghosts wouldn't come back, but, at the same time, Willow thought that might be the case. Sometimes ghosts just vanish into thin air and never come back.

And that just might be the case here. Willow burned a candle and meditated so she could figure out what happened with the two ghosts.

The answer came back to her - they were gone. For whatever reason, they were no longer in the atmosphere around Willow.

Willow took a deep breath and then called Nancy.

"Hey," Nancy said when Willow called her. "What's going on, Willow?"

"I've got a problem. Zelda is gone."

Nancy had originally hired Willow to be the ghostwriter for the Zelda Fitzgerald biopic because, at that time, Willow was being haunted by Zelda. Nancy had no desire to write the screenplay herself because she was extremely busy with some other projects and wasn't interested in the subject. She told Willow that she had no desire to learn more about the Fitzgeralds, the ultimate jazz-age couple who were the toast of New York before both of them started drinking too much, partying too much, and Zelda had a mental breakdown that saw her go into the mental hospital, where she died.

So, when Willow went to Nancy to offer her services to ghostwrite this screenplay, Nancy jumped at the chance.

And now, Willow was under a contract to get it done for Nancy. She couldn't just back out and not write the screenplay because if she did, that would mean she would be in breach of contract. And if there was one thing she didn't want to do, that was going to court for any reason at all. Not that anybody liked to go to court, but Willow intensely disliked it. And, she had no defense if she backed out.

Willow could try to tell the judge if she went to court that circumstances changed when Zelda disappeared, but she didn't imagine the judge would buy that. To say the least.

"Zelda is gone? Where did she go?" Nancy asked.

"Hell, I don't know. All I know is that I woke up this morning, she was no longer around, and I don't know what happened. Sometimes that happens. Sometimes ghosts want to stick around, but they don't. I don't really know exactly what happens in the spirit world. But I've had this happen to me before. The ghost appears, haunts you for a while, and then leaves. At any rate, I don't think I can do the screenplay."

Willow squeezed her eyes shut as she thought about what Nancy would say to her. After all, if Willow didn't have Zelda to help her with the screenplay, she wouldn't do a good job of it. And Nancy would have to put her name on Willow's work because Willow was only hired as a ghostwriter. So, Willow believed it would be in Nancy's best interest to go ahead and let her off the project.

"I'm sorry, Willow, but you agreed to do the screenplay, and I'm going to hold you to it. I'm extremely stressed out right now, and I can't deal with this. So, I don't know what to tell you. You signed a contract, and you'll have to write the screenplay."

Willow sighed. "Listen, you know what the deal is. I

told you. I've never written a screenplay in my life. And when I say never, I mean never. I'm not a writer. May I remind you that I'm the ghostwriter, and you are the actual writer, which means that if I screw this up, you're going to be the one whose reputation is going to be on the line."

"I'll take my chances," Nancy said and then hung up the phone.

Just what Willow feared. She was going to have to go ahead and write a screenplay based on the life of Zelda Fitzgerald, and she had no idea what she was doing.

"OK, Willow, you're gonna have to do it," she said to herself as she looked in the mirror at her reflection. "You've done things you were afraid of before, and you'll have to do this now. Besides, even if you write the crappiest screenplay ever, they're going to have script doctors who will fix it, and you're not going to be the one who'll be humiliated. That's going to be Nancy. She was the one who wasn't flexible enough to actually let you off this project even though the drawing card, the fact that Zelda Fitzgerald was hanging around eager to tell her story, is gone. So, go ahead, get a *Screenplay Writing For Dummies* book out of the library, and get going."

So, that's exactly what she did that day. She went to the library, got several books about writing screenplays, and went to work. This was not going to defeat her, and she would do the best job possible.

She might not have Zelda Fitzgerald around to actually tell her story, but Willow found several biographies on the woman. She also had a book about writing screenplays, along with Nancy's outline and treatment for the movie, and that would have to be enough.

She was ready. So, when Jackson came home for the

day, exhausted from all the meetings he had taken, Willow was already working hard on the computer.

Jackson still wasn't aware that Willow was the one who was going to be writing this screenplay for his very movie. So, Willow immediately shut the laptop when he came home.

She had no clue on how she was going to admit the truth about what she was doing, without Jackson thinking she was absolutely nuts.

Chapter Four

Sarah

Sarah was back on Nantucket, but only because she had to gather personal property together so that she could move out to California as soon as possible. At the moment, Julia, the young girl who would soon be her charge, was staying with her aunt Mary in Malibu. The two of them were grieving together the loss of Max, Julia's father and Mary's brother.

Sarah still felt shock about the entire thing with the death of Max. The way it all shook out was so unexpected that she still couldn't quite grasp that Max was gone.

At first, Max told Sarah he was dying and wanted to go to California and stay with his sister Mary to get residency out there. He needed residency in California because he would take advantage of California's right-to-die law. Max decided he would go out on his own terms.

At the time, Sarah had married him in Las Vegas, when

she was far from sober. Then again, maybe she married him because she really wanted to. *In vino veritas* and all that. But Max wanted to marry Sarah because he wanted her to become a stepmother for Julia. Sarah agreed to stay married to him for this reason, even though they married on a whim. Sarah was actually looking forward to being a mother to Julia. That was the one thing she'd always wanted: to have a child. She never got that chance, which was her greatest regret. And now, with her plan to become Julia's caregiver, she would have a chance to have a child.

So, when Sarah went out to California with Max, she was going out there with the expectation that she was going to get to know Julia and Mary and she was going to spend Max's last months with him. Then Max got word from a new doctor, Dr. Quan, that there was a possibility that he could beat his cancer. All at once, there was a bit of hope in Sarah and Max's life.

But then Sarah started to get cold feet as she imagined she would stay married to the man she married on a whim. She was afraid of making another mistake in her life like she did with Nolan all those years ago. She felt guilty for feeling that way, however. What kind of woman would think of herself when the man she loved was battling deadly cancer?

But then Max had a massive stroke and died. And at that time, Sarah wasn't really prepared for it. She'd just gotten good news from Dr. Quan about the possibility that Max could live a long life. She was trying to process her feelings about that when she got the news in the middle of the night that Max had died.

So, because of how everything went down, Sarah felt more than a little off-kilter about the entire thing. She was prepared for him to die, and then she wasn't. And then he did. And she was still trying to process all of it.

She was nervous about her possible new life out in California. She wasn't quite clear exactly what she would do when out there, although she and Ava had spoken seriously about the possibility of opening up a new winery in the Santa Monica Mountains. Sarah loved the winery she'd visited while she was out in California. It was high in the hills, with a beautiful view of the ocean once you got up there. Sarah had fantasized about what she would do if she were the one who owned the winery. She imagined herself being the host of many great events in her winery. She'd be so excited to host wedding receptions, retreats, anniversary parties, etc.

One thing was for sure - Southern California was the perfect climate for growing grapes. It had the same climate profile as Sardinia or Sicily, two places Sarah loved to visit when she traveled the world with Nolan, her ex-boyfriend. California was known for its Chardonnay grapes, but they also had a lot of other grape varietals that grew well in hot and sunny climates that were extremely dry, such as the climate in Southern California.

Sarah knew she would do a good job growing grapes out there, and would do a great job running a winery. And it was something that would be a challenge for her.

That was one thing that Sarah realized about her life. For much of her life, she wasn't being challenged at all. In fact, the last time she felt a challenge was way back before she met Nolan, and she was working for a large architectural firm in Los Angeles. The work there was stimulating, and she could use the creative part of her brain, which she enjoyed. She was an intelligent woman, and, up until the time she met Nolan, she was a very independent woman. She had her own money, her own career, her own life. That all changed when she met Nolan and decided to become more or less an appendage for him.

A trophy wife, even though she was never actually his wife.

And she was with him for over 20 years. So, for over 20 years, he was nothing more than a handbag for a wealthy man. She was on his arm at parties and was somebody he liked to brag about to his friends. And she was so damn bored with that life. She wasn't bored when they were traveling, which they did during his summer and winter breaks, as Nolan was a professor at Cal State. He was also the heir to billions, which was why he had the money to have a ginormous beach house in Monterey and could take Sarah around the world. While they were traveling, she was stimulated. She really enjoyed traveling and loved to immerse herself in different cultures. She always did.

Then Nolan died, and Sarah ended up on Nantucket, working for Ava. Once again, she wasn't really challenged. Her job for Ava consisted of purchasing wine for Ava's bed and breakfast and recommending wine to the people who came to stay with Ava. When needed, she pitched in with running the place.

When she worked for Ava and was busy, she could take her mind off her issues. How her life went so wrong, and how things weren't turning out as she wanted them to. But, unfortunately, Nantucket was definitely a place where it was feast or famine. Either the place was hopping with thousands of people on the island, or it was extremely quiet, and nothing much was going on. It was busy for really only three months out of the year. The rest of the time, there weren't many people around. It was an island of only 10,000 people, 50,000 when things got going during the summer months.

So, Ava's bed and breakfast was dead for much of the year. Whereas during the summer months, she had a full house plus a waiting list for her seven bedrooms, after the summer was over, she could barely fill two rooms. Sarah was no longer needed during these months, although Ava tried to find places for her to fill in.

Now, Sarah was getting a chance to start her life all over again, for real. She was going to be caring for Julia, and she was going to hopefully start a new business venture with Ava.

In other words, she was going to be starting over completely again.

For the second time in less than two years.

She was busy packing when Quinn came to her door.

"Hey there," Quinn said with a big smile. "I was going to come by and see if you needed anything."

Sarah shook her head. "I'm overwhelmed. I hate moving. You know, you never understand how much crap you got until you start packing everything in boxes. And sometimes, I just want to leave everything behind in this house, leave the real estate agent to take care of it, and just go unencumbered. But, then again, that wouldn't be fair to the real estate agent or the possible new tenants to leave stuff behind. So it's not like I can really do that."

The funny thing was, Sarah had just moved into this new house. She'd just purchased all new furniture and décor for the place. And now she was going to be moving again. She was going to be moving her completely new furniture across the country.

Quinn started to laugh. "Ain't that the truth about not knowing how much junk you have until you start packing it.

Anyhow, I wanted to stop by and lend a hand. I'm sure that Hallie and Ava will also be over here soon. Although Ava is currently in Brooklyn talking to Esther, the wife of Ava's birth father. But she'll be along as soon as she returns to the island."

Sarah smiled. She knew she'd have to help Quinn move as well. And that was going to be a real pain in the ass, even more so than Sarah's move, because Quinn had more stuff and a 13-year-old girl under her roof.

Sarah went to the back door, where her dog, Bella, was sitting patiently. Bella was a beautiful Pitbull mix who had been Sarah's rock for years. She imagined the dog romping on the beach in California, and she had to smile.

While she was in California, Bella stayed with Quinn, who had her own dog named Kona. Bella and Kona really got along quite well. Kona was supposedly a cross between a pug and a shepherd, and she was the sweetest dog in the world. Kona and Bella got along famously.

Sarah just shrugged her shoulders. "Thanks a lot for coming by, and you know I'll do the same for you when it's your turn.

At that, she handed Quinn a tape gun and some boxes. "Start in the kitchen. Just throw everything in there. I'll sort it out later when we get to California."

Quinn gave Sarah a salute and then got to work.

"By the way," Quinn said as she worked in the kitchen, carefully packing plates and glasses after wrapping them up in newspaper and then carefully placing them in a box. "I've been kind of thinking about the move. You and I will have 13-year-old girls we'll be caring for under our roofs. And they're best friends. I know this will sound kind of odd because, you know, we're in our mid-50s by now. But what would you think about the two of us getting a house together? We're both going to be working a lot, but maybe we're not going to have the same hours. After all, I'll be working days, and if you get that winery with Ava, you'll be working a lot of nights. It would be nice if somebody was always around to care for those two girls. And, if we're both not going to be around, we can hire a temporary nanny. Not that the girls really need supervision because they are 13 years old, but at the same time, I'd feel a lot more comfortable knowing there was an adult at home at all times."

Sarah, who was standing in the living room packing up some books in magazines, looked at Quinn. "That's kind of an amazing idea, actually. To tell you the truth, I was a little intimidated about moving out to California because I'm not going to have a lot of money to buy my own house. I mean, I'll probably get about 3 million for this house when all is said and done. That's not enough to buy a beach house in California at all. Especially not one on Venice Beach or Malibu, where Ava wants to go."

Of course, Sarah always had the option to take out a mortgage for a new home, just like millions of Americans do every year. But she didn't like the idea of having that big of a debt. She wanted to pay cash for a home and be done with it. But she didn't think she'd be able to do that.

But maybe if she lived with Quinn, she could get a nice beach house. After all, Quinn was doing quite well with her business. She was an interior designer. She did extremely well in New York City and continued to do well on Nantucket. Sarah knew Quinn was already making contacts in the Los Angeles area and had promising leads on some jobs she could start once she got out there. So there was every indication that Quinn would be just as successful in Los Angeles as in Nantucket or New York City. So, Quinn could put a substantial amount towards a new house, and so could Sarah, so between the two of them, they might be able to get something very nice.

Quinn also made a good point when she said they might have different work shifts. Sarah worried about who would look after Julia while she was working. And Quinn was correct that she probably would be working many evenings. Especially on the weekends. It was also a good point that if both of them worked during the day, they could pool their resources and get a nanny for their two children.

"I'm kind of loving this idea," Sarah said to Quinn. "I think it could really work out well for us."

"I do too," Quinn said. "I've been thinking a lot about it, and I've been trying to figure out what I was going to do with my Emerson. She's going to be going to school at that Los Angeles high school for the arts, which is going to be one hell of a bad drive from Venice Beach every day. I've already arranged for someone to take her there and pick her up, but sometimes I work weird hours. And you do too, or you will be. I just think it would be the ideal solution for both of us. And not only that, but our dogs love each other, so that's an added bonus."

Sarah had never even thought about the possibility of getting a house with Quinn, but she was really warming up to the idea now. "You know, that makes a lot of sense. And I did love the houses in the Venice Beach area. I never thought I'd be able to afford one of them, but we can probably get a nice one between the two of us."

Quinn gave Sarah an impulsive hug. "I think that's a great idea. And, by the way, I also wanted to ask you how you're holding up."

Sarah shrugged her shoulders. She didn't know how to express her feelings about Max dying. "It's a tough time for me. But I think it was the loss of the idea of him for me. I didn't really know him all that well. But I had it in my head that he and I were falling in love at the time when he died. So it's almost like I'm grieving the potential of what we could have had. But it's not quite as hard as it could be because Max was not woven into the fabric of my life. You know what I mean?"

Quinn was now going through the silverware and tossing various forks, knives and spoons into a box. "I do understand, sugar. More than you know. My brother James died many years ago. And I felt this hole in my life that I didn't think would ever be filled. He was part of the fabric of my life because we talked every day and saw each other as much as possible. I lived in New York City when he died, and he was living in Atlanta. So we didn't see each other a whole lot, but we talked a lot. And after he died, I missed my talks with him so much. I kept wanting to pick up the phone and call him. And then I wondered if it would have been more or less difficult if I had not been as close to him as I was. Maybe if I didn't talk to him every day but talked to him every six months or so, it wouldn't be as hard for me to lose him. But that's the thing about caring about people. You're going to lose some along the way. The only way to avoid that is to not get close to anybody, but then what kind of life is that?"

Sarah smiled wanly. "Yeah, I know what you're saying. My ex-boyfriend, Nolan, died when I was with him. And I felt so little about it that I felt guilty that I didn't feel since intense grief when he passed. But that was because a part of me felt like he was my captor and I was his prisoner. For many years I felt that way. So, when he died, I felt like my prison guard had died, and I felt guilty for feeling that way. But his death was somewhat easy for me, in the end, because I didn't go through any kind of intense grieving for him. Now I'm waiting for the grief to start with Max, and maybe it will. But right now I'm just so focused on getting back to California, taking custody of Julia and starting my life over again that I don't really think about much else."

Quinn nodded. "It's entirely possible you're still in shock or in the denial part of the grieving process. Or maybe it's just that you'll be OK with this situation. How is Julia doing?"

"Julia is doing great. I've talked to Mary daily, and they're surfing and hanging out every day. Of course, after school starts, everything is going to be cattywampus. As far as how Julia is doing emotionally, Mary says she's hanging in there. I feel so badly for her. She never knew her mother, and now her father is dead, and now she's going to be living with me, a woman who is still a perfect stranger to her. It seems like life is not giving that poor girl a break."

Quinn had moved on to the wine glasses, and she was very carefully wrapping them up and putting them into a box. "Oh, I hear that. Don't forget, I have a 13-year-old girl under my roof who hasn't exactly had the breaks in life, either. Emerson is a handful because she's so strong-willed. But I think Julia might be a lot easier to raise than Emerson. She doesn't seem like she's quite as much of a rebel as my young Emerson."

Yes, that was true. Emerson was definitely a handful, and it seemed that Julia wouldn't be as much trouble as Emerson was to Quinn when she first came to her. Julia was quiet, respectful, and a bit introverted. There was no question about why Emerson and Julia were such good friends - they were opposites, and opposites attract. Emerson's in-your-face attitude attracted Julius's quiet nature, and

Emerson probably needed somebody like Julia to ground her just a bit.

"I think I can agree with you there. Emerson definitely has a mind of her own, but thank God for that. She's so socially conscious and aware. She was the one who inspired me to run for the school board, and now here I am, dropping that endeavor to move across the country."

Sarah was feeling kind of bad about that dropping her school board bid. After all, she was getting people involved with her school board campaign. The wife of a billionaire held a big fundraiser for her. She had people who had donated to her campaign. And now she'd have to pay them all back because she wouldn't be running anymore. She knew she had a good reason for abandoning the school board thing, but that didn't mean she didn't feel guilty about doing it. Just for once, she wanted to see something through to the end. And so far, she hadn't really had that chance.

Quinn nodded as she moved over to the tea cups and the bowls. "By the way, you have really pretty things," she said, admiring the floral prints on Sarah's dishes and bowls. "Where did you get these?"

"In Italy. I bought a full set in Positano and then had it shipped to my home in Monterey. You know, when I moved out here, that's all I really had to my name. Things like these bowls and the glasses you just wrapped up. Souvenirs from around the world. I didn't have a whole lot when I moved out here. So it wasn't nearly as overwhelming to move from Monterey to here as it's going to be to go in reverse."

Sarah moved over to the fireplace area of the living room, where some beautiful artifacts from around the world were carefully arranged. Quinn was still busy in the kitchen.

"I know what you're saying about Emerson," Quinn said. "It's true that while she's a handful, she inspires me with her passion. Everything in her life is like an 11 on a scale of 1 to 10. Both bad and good. But the good thing about that is she sees problems out in the world and wants to try fixing them. Even if she's just one voice, a virtual grain of sand on the beach, she doesn't care. She has the attitude that even if she's just a grain of sand on that beach, if every other grain of sand could just come together, they could make an entire beach. So that's what she tries to do - she tries to get people to join her causes. And I love that about her because she's such a leader. When I was her age, I just complained about the world. She really gets in there and does things about it."

Sarah just realized that she was going to be getting two for the price of one, in a way. She was going to not only be raising Julia, but she was going to be helping to raise Emerson. And that prospect really made her heart soar. All this time, all she wanted in her life was to be able to raise a child. And now, she was going to help raise two.

"Quinn, I can't tell you how excited this move makes me," Sarah said. "California is my home, and it has been for three decades or so. But, I'm also looking forward to becoming a family unit with you, Emerson, Julia, and me. It's just a very exciting new chapter of my life that's coming up. I don't really know what's going to be around the corner. None of us do. But I know that I want to experience life in the sun. The year-round sun, except for when it's May Grey and June Gloom, of course." Sarah was referring to the relentless overcast days that marked much of May and June in southern California. Most of the grey burns off by noon, however, and the sun comes out, so the May Grey and June Gloom characterizations weren't entirely accurate.

Quinn started to laugh. "May Grey and June Gloom. It's funny that you guys think it's bad weather when it's overcast and grey for two months out of the year. The rest of us consider bad weather to be 10 feet of snow piled up outside our door. There's one beautiful thing about this move - in California, I'm not going to have to shovel snow. I'll not have to go out to my car with inch-thick ice on the windshield and pour hot water on the ice to melt it. You know, that's a dangerous thing to do, but I didn't care. It was a lot better than having to scrape it with the scraper."

Sarah sat down at the fireplace because she needed to take a little break. "What do you mean it's dangerous to pour hot water on an icy windshield? When I went to school in Kansas, I used to do that kind of thing all the time." Sarah had to smile when she thought about her college days in Lawrence, Kansas. The winters were brutal in the Midwest, and Sarah didn't have a garage for her car or even a carport. There was more than one morning when she was late for class, and it snowed the night before, sometimes out of nowhere. And, of course, with the snow came the inch-thick ice on the windshield. Sarah would boil a tea kettle of water and pour it on the windshield. She never heard that was a bad thing to do.

"Sugar, here's the thing. Anytime you combine hot water with cold glass, you're in danger of that glass breaking. Of course, it's a lot harder to break a windshield with hot water than, say, pouring boiling water into a drinking glass. But, it's been known to happen."

"Makes sense," Sarah said. "I guess I never really thought of it that way."

The two ladies worked together for several hours. By the time midnight rolled around, Sarah had much of her house packed up with the help of Quinn. They toasted their accomplishment with a glass of wine, and Quinn went home. "Emerson isn't home. She's staying with her friend tonight. But it's getting late, and I really should skedaddle. I'm really happy we're going to be sharing a house. And I know that you and I will have very similar tastes when it comes to a house. So, we should start looking for a place when we move to California."

"Yes. That'll be good."

Chapter Five

Hallie

Hallie was feeling excited about the move to California. Although she was settled there on Nantucket, she missed her daughter Morgan. She and Morgan had grown fairly close in the past couple of years since Hallie found her own life and stopped smothering her daughter. And now Morgan was also living in Los Angeles, having sold her art gallery in San Francisco. So Hallie would be able to see her daughter a lot more often.

Of course, Hallie being Hallie, she worried a lot about how things would go once she got out there. At the moment, she was part owner of this wonderful Nantucket spa named for her business partner, Willow. She was still working on getting an online degree in nutrition, so she could offer that to the spa clients. She was very close to completing the online course, and she was very close to getting her certification in integrative nutrition.

But there was one person she was really going to miss on Nantucket, and that was Conrad Maxwell.

Conrad was an artist there on the island. Hallie had been working for him for the past few months, mainly helping him boost his self-confidence. That was one of the things that she did for people in her life coaching business - she made them drill down and see their own potential. It wasn't always easy to do. A lot of people had a bit of a mental block when it came to their own successes. And Hallie found that with many people, including herself, it was much easier to listen to the negative feedback in life than the positive one. All the people who put you down come and make you feel like 2 inches tall, all the people who count you out - those seemed to be the people that were listened to. The people who were on your side, give you praise, say encouraging words - those are the people who get discounted.

Hallie knew that, for instance, if Ava said something nice to her, she would hear the words but not absorb them because it was coming from Ava, who was biased because Ava loved Hallie so much. But if Hallie heard something negative coming from somebody, even somebody she didn't know, she'd take that criticism to heart, and it would wound her. She would assume the criticism was correct and any kind of praise was not. That was a function of her low self-esteem, but she also found that it was a bit of a human nature trait.

She was starting to feel better about herself. She had such low self-esteem before because, well, she hadn't had very many successes in her life. She'd failed at every job she'd ever tried, she was in a toxic marriage and her daughter shunned her. So, when she came out to Nantucket, she felt like a failure. All the way around. It was only through Willow putting her through acupuncture, which, as Willow explained, opened up the energy centers in her body, that Hallie started to feel better about herself. And she started to think she could help other people with similar self-doubts she had in her life.

Which led her to Conrad Maxwell. He was a successful and very talented artist, but he constantly had a sense of self-doubt. She worked hard to make him see that he was talented and had a lot of fans. It was very difficult to get him to that place. It took a lot of not just talking him through his negative thoughts and replacing them with positive ones but also a lot of organization in his life. And, through it all, she'd actually became friends with the man.

She even came to have a few romantic feelings for him. However, she never thought he'd feel the same way about her. Conrad was from England and had a very sexy British accent and a British way of talking about things. Hallie loved to listen to him speak. Just the terms he used that were foreign to her were music to her ears. When he'd talk about fancying things, lighting a fag, or referring to friends of his as mates, Hallie loved listening to him talk. Hallie laughed internally whenever he said something about bumming a fag from somebody.

So she was definitely going to miss the guy. And that day, she was scheduled to meet with him. She was going down to his studio because they were supposed to go to a party later that night. It was a party held by a wealthy patron with a beach house on the island who was going to give Conrad a large grant to keep working on his art.

She walked to his studio from her hotel room. She'd been staying at an extended stay place since she got on the island because she just never wanted to find a place to live. She also stayed with Quinn for awhile because she was battling cancer, but, after she beat the cancer, she moved back to the extended stay place because she didn't want to be in the way. She knew that the itinerant way she was living would probably not last, and indeed, it wasn't going to because she would hopefully be moving out to Los Angeles with her friends.

When she got to Conrad's studio, he was enjoying a glass of whiskey. His long grey hair was pulled into a pony-tail. That was usually how she saw him - with a man bun or ponytail. His blue eyes were always twinkling with mischief and mirth. And, even though he was prone to depression, as many artists were, he always had a smile on his face. Even when he was depressed, he was funny. In fact, sometimes, when he was depressed, he was even funnier than usual. That was because when he was depressed, his cynicism came out and his cynicism was often hilarious.

"Hello, Hallie," he said in a sing-song voice as he sat in a chair and drank his whiskey. "This is really the hair of the dog because last night, I drank way too much and passed out. I got so pissed. I'm glad you weren't around."

Hallie knew the term "pissed" meant drunk, unlike the word in the American English language. That was always something that was difficult for Hallie to interpret. So, when he said he got pissed, he wasn't angry, he was just rip-roaring drunk.

"Well, Conrad, you look pretty good for having tied one on last night. What was the occasion?" Hallie was afraid he would say something about having been on a date. If he said that, she didn't think she'd be able to take it because she was starting to like him romantically.

"Do I have to have a special occasion to enjoy a cock-tail?" Conrad laughed a little bit and then took another sip of his whiskey. "Don't answer that question. Anyhow, how are you?"

"I'm doing really well," Hallie said. "I'm moving out to Los Angeles. I'm thinking about moving to the Venice Beach area with my friends Sarah and Quinn. I mean, we're not going to live together, they're going to live together, but I'm gonna get a place of my own. And Ava is looking to get a house in Malibu. Ava really likes how the houses there are right on the beach. She likes to hear ocean waves coming in while she's sleeping."

"Los Angeles, huh?" Conrad said with a twinkle in his blue eyes. "You gonna go out there and get your boobs done? That's a requirement out there, you know. I think you're required to get at least one thing done a year. Your nose, your ass, your boobs. Unless, of course, you just want to go and get Botox all the time. Not that you need Botox. You look fine just the way you are."

Hallie felt herself blushing. Did Conrad find her attractive? She had no idea. Him telling her she looked fine just the way she was was the closest he'd come to saying he found her attractive.

"I know you're joking, Conrad. But you're not far wrong. I think plastic surgery is a booming business out there, to say the very least. But don't worry, I don't plan to get anything done when I get there. Maybe I have a few extra wrinkles and just a little bit of junk in my trunk, but I've earned every one of those wrinkles and every pound of the junk in my trunk. So don't worry. I'm not going to immediately go for Botox and liposuction just because I'll be living in the Los Angeles area."

Conrad was looking at her with a cock of his head. "Yeah, of course, I'm joking. I always try to make a joke when I'm gutted."

Hallie bit her bottom lip. Conrad just said he would be gutted because she would be moving across the country? She wondered what he was getting at.

Hallie sat next to him. "Maybe I can have a shot of your whiskey?"

"Of course," he said. "It's peanut butter whiskey. It's smooth. I discovered it when I went to a bar one night, and they had it. The bartender recommended it, and it was love at first sip."

Hallie took the shot glass full of the amber liquid and downed it. Conrad was right. It was very smooth and tasted almost buttery. Peanut buttery. Which was appropriate, considering it was peanut butter whiskey.

Conrad put his arm around her. "So, you're going to move out to Los Angeles. I don't suppose you could fit me in your suitcase? You know there are a lot of art galleries out in that area. Los Angeles is a booming city for the arts these days. It's always a place I love to visit. I mean, yeah, there are a lot of wankers running around the beach thinking they're the cock of the walk when they're lamer than dirt. And there are a lot of lasses walking around thinking their shit don't stink. But it's still a pretty laid-back place. I think I could be happy out there."

Hallie felt her heart racing. She wanted him to move out there. She thought he'd have a lot more opportunity in Los Angeles than there on Nantucket. To say the very least. She knew if they went out there together, he would immerse himself in the arts community out there, and he'd be very happy.

Yet, she was very shy about asking him to go with her. She thought he would have definitely turned her down. She swallowed hard.

"Would you really move out to LA?" Hallie asked him.

"Would it seem like I'm following you if I did?" he asked. "I don't want it to be weird. But yeah, I'd love to go to live in Los Angeles. I've thought about it from time to time. I looked at empty gallery spaces out there, and I fell in love with one space. Hardwood floors, exposed brick, 30-foot ceilings. I really fancied that place."

All at once, Hallie felt incredibly nervous. To tell the truth, she had a crush on Conrad, and had for some time. But she never imagined in 400 million years that he would feel the same way about her. But apparently, he did. At least, judging by the way he was looking at her, he did.

"It'd be fun if you lived in Los Angeles, too," Hallie said. "My daughter Morgan is out there. As you know, she's a well-known artist. I could introduce you."

Conrad grinned. "Your daughter is out in LA now? I thought she was in San Francisco."

"Morgan moved out to Los Angeles just last month, as a matter of fact. She said there was more opportunity in Los Angeles and a more vibrant art community than in San Francisco. After all, LA does have more galleries than any other city besides New York."

"Do you think Morgan and I would get on? The gallery that she has in LA, what kind of artists does it feature?"

Conrad tended to dabble in a little bit of Neo-Dadaism, some protest art, and a little bit of Neo-Surrealism. He was influenced by Dada artists in the 1920s, such as Hannah Hoch, Hans Richter and Marcel Duchamp. His surrealist influences were Salvador Dali, Francis Bacon, Joan Miró and Max Ernst.

"Her gallery is currently looking for all kinds of different artists. I'm sure there'll be a wing that could showcase artists who are Neo-Dada and Neo-Surreal. And yes, I think you and my daughter would get on."

Conrad nodded his head. "Well, if I decided to pop on over to Los Angeles myself, would it be weird for you? I mean, I certainly don't want you to think you're obligated to take me on as your pet project or anything like that."

Hallie looked around Conrad's studio, which was in the historic district of Nantucket. She knew Conrad owned the studio and the land it was on, so it was probably quite valuable to him. As with Ava, if he decided to go ahead and sell his gallery, he could get a pretty penny off of that. In fact, he could probably get enough from his gallery there on Nantucket to buy his own gallery in LA.

He would be a small fish in Los Angeles, as opposed to a big fish in a small town such as Nantucket. Yet, Hallie could see Conrad thriving in a much bigger city. And, since Morgan had made a lot of contacts in the Los Angeles art world and made many friends in LA, she certainly could help Conrad get a leg up on making his own friends in that world. He wouldn't be going to Los Angeles on a wing and a prayer without a plan.

"Well, what the hell," Hallie said. "Why don't you come on out to Los Angeles, too? Morgan was considering creating an art cooperative. I could certainly talk to her and see if she'd be open to inviting you into the cooperative if she does that. I think that would be a really great idea. It's for one of the galleries that she's gonna be opening in the Venice Beach area, actually. Which is where I plan on maybe getting a home."

Conrad nodded his head. "That sounds like a really good idea. I'd be chuffed about such a thing. I love living on this island, don't get me wrong. There's something about being by the water that's very comforting for me. You know, I lived in London before I came here. Cold, rainy, nowhere near the sea. I loved going to Brighton whenever I could.

My mum and dad had a twee little cottage out there right on the water. We used to go there every summer for a month while my dad was on holiday from his job. He was a lorry driver, and he got six weeks off every year, and we'd go to Brighton and just hang about. It was like going to the carnival every year for me."

Conrad's blue eyes had the familiar twinkle in them but also a hint of sadness. That was something that was often behind the smiles – nostalgia and longing to be with one's parents again. Once you got to be their age, most of their peers no longer had parents. They were a generation of orphans, in a way. And Conrad was no different. His parents had both been dead for the past 20 years.

His father had been prone to depression and, like Conrad, was extremely artistically inclined. He might've been a truck driver, but he was always an artist in his heart. Conrad felt his father's depression came from the fact that he was an artist behind the wheel of a truck and how that ground down on him. After seeing his father go into black depressions and drink himself into an early grave, Conrad swore he would not be like him. In other words, Conrad decided at a young age that he wouldn't be just a cog in the wheel who did art on the side like his father was. He was going to make a living off his art, come hell or high water, and thankfully he had the talent and drive to get it done.

Unfortunately, the art world was not a place where you could sit on your laurels. You could never take your foot off the gas in that world. It was too much of a competitive field, and you really had to have an abundance of talent, a visionary eye for what's up-and-coming, and an originality that set you apart from everybody else. That was very difficult to do. The result was that Conrad perpetually felt he was under a lot of pressure to produce highly original work.

He was constantly afraid that he was a derivative hack and people would see through him. That was one of the things that Hallie had helped him overcome – that sense of self-doubt.

"Well, since you love living by the water so much, you can certainly do that in Venice Beach," Hallie said. "That's where I'm going to be living, I think. So will Quinn and Sarah because they're going to be getting a place together so they can watch each other's children."

Conrad grinned. "We could get a place out there together. We could be flatmates. What do you think about that? I could get the top half of the house, and you can get the bottom half."

Hallie looked at Conrad, trying to figure out what he was thinking. So far, he hadn't made any kind of romantic overtures toward her. So, there wasn't any reason to think Conrad's offer to share a house with her would be anything other than a platonic situation. Flatmates, as he said. And Hallie thought that would be a pretty good idea, considering Conrad would be able to bring considerable wealth into the situation. She, herself, had some money in the bank, money she got from her divorce settlement, but she didn't think it was enough money to actually buy a house on Venice Beach herself.

"Conrad, I think that's a wonderful idea. Do you think we can get along?"

Conrad nodded his head. "Again, I don't want you to think this whole thing is just too weird. But I don't think I told you how much you've helped me these past few months. I was in a pit, just blackness that I couldn't see out of. I didn't want to work because I didn't think I was good enough. I thought I was just such a hack, such a toad. But you cared enough to see what I was going through, and you helped me. So, yes, I think we can get on quite well, even living together. We just need to give each other our space. You know, you want to have blokes over, and I can make myself scarce."

Hallie smiled, but her heart sunk just a little bit. Conrad was implying that she was just a friend, and, what's more, she was more like a security blanket than anything else. There was no way he would even joke about her having a bloke over if he was interested in her romantically. Not that she minded helping him. She really enjoyed helping people. It was her calling. She had a knack for drilling down on a person's issue, what their mental block was, and helping people overcome it.

"Okay. Sounds like a plan," Hallie said. "At the moment, I really am not encumbered by much. I could just move out to California without worrying about packing up anything except for my clothes and some books. I don't have any furniture here. That's the advantage of living itinerantly, as I have been doing here – when you want to pack up and leave, you can pack up and leave and not have to worry about getting a truck to haul your stuff out."

Truth be told, Hallie didn't bother with finding a place there on Nantucket because she was too focused on battling her cancer. She didn't want to take anything away from that, so she didn't bother to look for a new house and, in fact, stayed with Quinn while she was getting treatment. Moving felt overwhelming to her, especially when she was undergoing chemotherapy.

Now she was happy she decided to stay at the extended stay hotel instead of trying to find a home. Because now, she would be able to settle down, maybe create some roots, in the Venice Beach area. And she was now eager to do just that. She was looking forward to finding a home in the

Venice Canal area, where the pepper and eucalyptus trees lined a water canal.

"Okay, then, it's settled," Hallie said. "We're going to go to California and live as flatmates."

Conrad handed her a shot of whiskey, and she downed it. And then he poured her another shot, and they clinked their shot glasses together before she downed another one. The peanut butter whiskey was so smooth going down her throat. It felt good to be able to do this because while she was doing her chemotherapy, she wasn't drinking. Even when she got together with her ladies, and they inevitably had a bottle of wine to split between them, Hallie didn't drink.

But now, she was able to drink, and she felt liberated.

At some point, however, Hallie was aware that she would be in danger of losing control if she drank anymore. She was always able to talk to herself when she started to drink and tell herself that she had to quit drinking at a certain time or else she would act a fool. And if there was one thing that Hallie never did was lose control and start acting a fool.

So, after several more shots, she just smiled at Conrad. "Well, future roommate, let's go to this fundraiser."

They went to the fundraiser and had a blast.

And afterward, as Hallie lay in her bed in her hotel room, she thought about what would come up.

Her life was about to change, and she couldn't be more excited.

Chapter Six

Ava

Eight Weeks Later (End of June)

Everything moved very smoothly, and before Ava knew it, she had the deed to her Nantucket home in her hand, and she could sell it on the open market. And with the money she got for the sale of her home, she could purchase the beach home of her dreams in Malibu.

The Malibu State Lagoon Beach was a combination of a state park and residential beach, where people could walk along the dusty trail that encircled a lagoon. The trail was lined by enormous pine, sycamore, and pepper trees, which were Ava's favorite trees because they strongly resembled the willow trees she always loved.

When Ava was growing up, there was an old willow tree close to the house where she lived, and she was a bit of a tomboy, so she loved to climb that tree. The branches were very close together, and they started very low on the tree, so it was really an easy tree to climb. She would climb to the top, then would get scared and wouldn't know if she could come down. When she was at the top of the tree, she would imagine that, eventually, the fire department would have to be called, and she'd have to be saved. However, she would come down at some point, having conquered her fear. Then the very next day, she would do it all again, complete with the fear of not knowing if she was going to be able to come down.

Now, by the house in California, there were the ubiquitous pepper trees that were, to Ava's eye, identical to the willow trees. They had the same branch structure and the same hanging leaves. The only difference was that they had little red peppers growing on the branches that were used to make pink peppercorns. Ava loved the flavor of the California peppercorns. They were spicy and sweet and always imparted a distinct flavor to the food.

Ava's new home, which was directly on the beach, was a Tudor-style home with four bedrooms and an enormous deck that Ava fell in love with. She moved into this home one week ago and was still very busy unpacking boxes.

And there were so.many.boxes. Boxes of books, boxes of knickknacks, boxes of clothes, boxes of plates and glasses and cups. Boxes that she didn't know what they would contain because, towards the end, she didn't exactly label everything. So there was more than once when she would get to a box and not know exactly what was in there, and then would be pleasantly surprised that it was something that she didn't know she still had.

Sarah and Quinn had found a beautiful old home built in the 1920s and had enough bedrooms for the four of them – Quinn, Sarah, Emerson, and Julia – with a couple of bedrooms to spare. When Sarah and Quinn found the place, Quinn immediately drew up plans to work her interior decorating magic. The place would be a showroom when it was done.

Hallie and Conrad found their own home in the Venice Beach area, but theirs was a more modern style, inspired by the great architect Frank Lloyd Wright. Their home was all geometric angles, huge windows, and brick. As with Sarah and Quinn's home, Hallie and Conrad's new place was on the banks of a canal. In their front yard were a pepper tree, a pine tree, a bush bougainvillea, and several succulents. Succulents were the most prominent plant in California because of the perpetually dry weather in the Golden State.

Ava was able to sell her house on Nantucket for enough money that she was able to buy the Malibu house with money to spare. A winery was for sale, high up in the Santa Monica Mountains. Sarah and Ava put a bid on the winery, and they were able to win that particular bid. So, as soon as everybody moved into their homes, Sarah and Ava were going to go to their new winery and start working there.

It was only June, so it was early in the growing season. Grapes in California generally were not ready for harvesting until July, and the season went from July to October. So, Ava and Sarah were going to check out the grounds, see what needed to be done, and get a liquor license because they needed to open up a tasting room. So far, this particular winery bottled wines to send to distributors and hadn't opened a tasting room yet. That was going to be what Ava would work on – getting a license to sell liquor there on the premises.

She was finally unpacked, so she felt it was time to relax and have a bottle of wine. She went out to her deck and sat on a chair, listening to the waves. On the Malibu Lagoon

State Beach, when the sun set, it set behind the Santa Monica Mountains bordering Malibu. That was the beautiful thing about this particular part of California, Malibu – you got to take advantage of the beach and the hills that rose up behind you.

She smiled as she saw dogs romping on the beach, chasing after bones, and each other, snarling at each other playfully. Ava had decided that she should get a couple of dogs of her own. She was going to get two dogs, not one because she never wanted animals to be alone all day. She wanted all animals to have playmates.

While living on Nantucket, she was hesitant to get a pet because she was running a bed and breakfast and didn't know if the people staying with her would be allergic to dogs. But now that she was in Malibu and living in this house, she felt free. She felt like she didn't have to entertain people there anymore, which was liberating. And she felt she could get dogs without worrying about anybody complaining about it.

And, once she got out on the beach and settled in a bit, she would call her half-brother Elijah. Well, actually, he was merely her stepbrother, not her half-brother. After all, she and Elijah didn't have any parents in common, and they were in the same boat. They both were a part of a family, but not really part of the family. In Ava's case, she was never part of that family at all. Except that she kind of was, in a way. It was still very confusing for her.

But Elijah was a part of the fabric of the family. Yet, Ava wondered if he felt a bit alienated. His half-sisters, Rachel and Deborah, knew the secret about his birth. They understood that Elijah had a different father from them. This was something that Esther and James apparently told them years ago. Unlike her mother, they could talk about such serious issues in the Bloch family. That was one thing she understood when she talked to Esther: there was never a secret about who Elijah belonged to.

Ava was intensely curious about how Elijah felt about all of that and if he knew about her. Surprisingly enough, according to Esther, Rachel and Deborah never knew there was another kid in the woodwork. They never knew their father had sired another child while he married their mother. They only knew that Elijah was their half-brother.

Esther didn't go into a lot about what happened when Elijah was born. Rachel and Deborah were four and five years old when Elijah was born. Esther didn't talk about how Elijah coped with the knowledge that the man who gave him his DNA was not the same man he was looking at around the dinner table every night.

Ava wondered if Elijah felt the same way she did. Ever since she discovered that her father wasn't Kenny, the man Ava always thought was her father, Ava felt just a little bit lost. Like half of her was missing and could never be restored. She was starting to fill in the blanks just a little bit with her birth and with her conversations with Esther. And now, she was anxious to talk to Elijah and learn more about living in that family and how James was as a day-to-day father. And she was also extremely anxious to know how he dealt with the knowledge that he was essentially born out of wedlock.

So, Ava sat on the enormous deck facing the water and nervously dialed Elijah's number. Esther had assured her that Elijah was expecting her call, but that didn't make her any less nervous. She was going to commiserate with the guy and hoped he'd be somebody she could become friends with.

He answered the phone, and she told him who she was.

"Ava," he said with a very friendly tone to his voice. "My mom told me you would probably get in touch with me when you came out here. I live in a condo out here in Tivoli Cove. Would you like to have dinner with me tonight? My treat. I know a great seafood place in Santa Monica. What do you say?"

Ava nodded her head but knew that this nonverbal communication was not going to translate over the phone. She remembered Carrie on *Sex and the City* doing the same thing, nodding on the phone and then explaining, "I'm nodding."

"Yes," she finally said to him. "I'd love to do that. What do you say, about 7 o'clock?"

"7 o'clock sounds great."

When she hung over the phone, she felt nervous again. She would find out all about her other family from this guy tonight. And she didn't really know what she would find out, which terrified her. But, never mind, she would face her fears about possibly finding out that James was not the man she thought she was. Then again, maybe he was going to tell her that James was a total mensch, the upstanding man she always knew he was when she had lunch with him.

She didn't really know what she was going to find out. And that was what was making her extremely nervous.

Chapter Seven

Willow

The weeks went by, and Willow gamely banged out the screenplay for the life of Zelda Fitzgerald without Zelda even making an appearance to try to correct the record. Willow had to rely on biographies, just like everybody else did. And that really frustrated her.

Hallie was now out here in California. And this meant that Willow's spa in Nantucket was closed down, even though, it being June, it was a busy season on the island. If she was on Nantucket, she'd be making money hand over fist because she always did. Her spa was extremely popular with the locals because it was unique in the services it offered. Willow was always astounded at the number of people who wanted alternative healing and wanted a little bit of magic with their healing. While the locals tended to love her spa, Willow found that, during the busy season, her business expanded exponentially through word of mouth from those same locals. So, Willow was losing a ton of money by being out in California when she should've been on Nantucket.

Willow was stuck out in California and was quite frustrated because she didn't think this screenplay would be very good. She met with Nancy once a week, and Nancy assured her that everything was going great. But Willow could catch the vibes off Nancy and realized Nancy was blowing smoke up her ass because she wanted Willow to stay on the project. Nancy didn't want to get sued for not completing the screenplay on her own, so she was desperate for Willow to produce a screenplay for Zelda Fitzgerald that Nancy could hand over to script doctors to work their magic.

In the meantime, Willow and Jackson were growing closer every day. Once Willow decided she would give him a chance, she could see him for what he was – he was a cool dude, extremely talented, and a very hard worker. Since the Zelda Fitzgerald project was in pre-production, Jackson's time was spent on the set getting fitted for costumes and meeting all the background workers. When he wasn't on the set, he was busy with his modeling gigs and going to acting classes. He even helped out with set design. Jackson had some knowledge about set design because he'd studied it on his own and had some good creative input for the set designers.

If there is one thing that Jackson hated about historical films, it was inaccuracies. For instance, an actual car drove in the background of *The Good the Bad and the Ugly*, a movie set during the Civil War. That was one thing that Jackson enjoyed showing Willow. She was astounded when she saw the car driving across the road about a thousand feet behind the head of Clint Eastwood as he was trying to blow up a bridge. Willow had no idea how something like that could happen – didn't the editor see that?

And once she saw bloopers like that, Jackson was eager to show her all kinds of other ones. For instance, in the movie *Titanic*, Rose admired paintings by Monet and Picasso, both of which were never on the ship in the first place and never sank. In fact, one of the paintings shown in that movie is currently hanging in the museum of modern art in New York City. And Willow always thought it was strange that, when Cal Hockley asked Rose who the artist was of a certain painting, Rose answered the words "something Picasso." By 1912, Picasso was already famous. Rose was an upper-class woman who was interested in art and would've known who he was. After all, he became famous around 1909 during his famed blue period, and she bought one of his paintings. So, Willow thought it was odd that Rose would refer to him as "something Picasso."

The biggest bloopers in all kinds of movies were the models and styles of cars being driven in certain historical films. For instance, they watched a movie set in 1925, and at least one or two cars weren't unavailable until 1929 or even later. Lamps and other light fixtures were not always correct, either. Sometimes certain telephones in a historical film weren't the models available during that time. There seemed to be a million and one of these anachronisms in historical movies, and, to an untrained eye like Willow, they weren't noticed. But Jackson had a trained eye for picayune details and was a history buff. He also knew a lot about car models and could easily spot car anachronisms. So, Jackson's expertise was sought-after on the Zelda Fitzgerald movie set, and he provided a second eye about things that might be out of place.

Willow personally thought it was all pretty hilarious. She

knew that every historical film had an army of consultants who would go through every prop on the set and ensure it was historically accurate. Yet, so many of these things got through the final film, and Willow wondered how any of that ever happened.

Then, one day, Jackson managed to catch Willow in the act of writing the screenplay for the movie he was going to star in. She kept the fact that she was writing the screenplay a secret from him because she couldn't explain exactly why she was doing it. She didn't want to admit to Jackson that she'd been haunted by two ghosts and that one of them, the ghost of Zelda Fitzgerald, had compelled her to write the screenplay. It was even more embarrassing to tell him about it now because Zelda was currently gone.

Jackson wasn't supposed to be home that day. He was supposed to have been on the set, meeting with the director and the cast and going in for more costume fittings. He came home that day, and Willow was hanging out in his apartment because she was staying with him for the time being. Her hotel room was just too expensive, and Jackson had invited her to stay with him while she was in town.

He came home, and she was in the zone, writing her screenplay, with books about Zelda Fitzgerald piled up around her. She was so in the zone that she didn't even notice he came in, and when he came up behind her and looked at what she was writing about, she jumped.

"What the hell are you doing home?" Willow demanded.

Jackson was looking at her with a funny look. "This is my apartment. Am I not allowed to come home? The meeting got over a lot earlier than I thought, and I wanted to see if you wanted to go out to eat tonight. But I come home, and you're working on what looks like a screenplay centered on Zelda Fitzgerald. What's going on?"

Willow took a deep breath. "Okay. You caught me. Here's the deal." Another deep breath. "There's a lot you don't know about me. One of the things you don't know about me is that I'm sensitive. And when I say the word sensitive, it means I occasionally am in touch with the spirit world."

"The spirit world," Jackson repeated, his face blank.

"You know, ghosts," Willow said. "And I came out here in the first place because the ghosts of Zelda Fitzgerald and Clara Bow haunted me into coming out here. And then, while talking to you, I realized you were up for a part in a movie about F. Scott Fitzgerald. Once I found out you were going for a part in that movie, Zelda Fitzgerald hounded me into writing the screenplay for your movie. And then, out of nowhere, the crazy broad disappeared." Willow took a deep breath. "There you go. Now you know your friend Willow is absolutely certifiably bat-crap crazy."

Jackson was looking at her with an expression that said he was thinking about her words and not ready to have her committed to a mental hospital. "Okay, the ghosts of Clara Bow and Zelda Fitzgerald haunted you into coming out here. And then Zelda Fitzgerald insisted that you write the screenplay about her life. And then she disappeared before she could dictate to you the screenplay?" He shook his head. "Why would Clara Bow be involved with this?"

"Hell if I know," Willow said to him. "I wondered that myself. All I know is that Zelda bullied me into writing the screenplay, and now she's nowhere to be found. And, there you have it. So, I'm stuck writing a screenplay as a ghost-writer for Nancy Tallow. I don't know what I'm doing. And the only thing I really want to do is to go back to Nantucket and get back to my spa and my life."

When she said that, Jackson looked like she had wounded him. "I see. Here I was hoping that you were out here to see me because you realized that we should be together."

"Yeah, sorry about that," Willow said. "Hate to burst your bubble, but I'm not interested in a relationship with you."

Jackson looked even more wounded. "You know, something happened when I met you at my mom's Christmas party," he said. "It's like I had this flash go through me, and I had a weird sensation of looking through the eons. Like I could, in a flash, see myself holding your hand through the centuries. It was the weirdest thing ever to feel that."

Willow knew what he was talking about. Because she knew, much better than he did, just how long she and Jackson went back. He was right. They had spent eons together. She'd experienced many past lives, over the course of centuries, millennia even, and, in every one of those lives, Jackson was next to her. She had a very good grasp of this knowledge.

Jackson, on the other hand, seemed to only have a fleeting glimpse of how strong his bond was with Willow. That was apparently enough for him to feel extremely attached to Willow, evidenced by the fact that he'd already essentially asked her to move in with him.

Willow didn't respond to Jackson talking about his flash at his mother's Christmas party when he met her. She didn't want to confirm to him they were soulmates. "Dude, that's the weirdest thing I've ever heard. But, whatever. Anyhow, I signed a contract with Nancy Tallow to ghostwrite the Zelda Fitzgerald biopic screenplay because I wanted to help

Zelda tell her story. Now she's gone. I'm stuck with writing the screenplay because I signed that contract with Nancy, and that's the only reason I'm still out in Los Angeles. So, there you have it. I'm bat-crap crazy, and I'm a sucker to boot. Trust me, you don't want to be involved with me."

When he looked at her, however, she knew she wouldn't be able to stand her ground with him. He took her hands and kissed her. She closed her eyes and felt electricity shoot through her body. No matter how often he kissed her, she felt the same amount of electricity. And that really unnerved her.

"Why don't you want to be involved with me?" he asked in a low voice after he kissed her.

Willow sighed. "Here's the thing. I don't do relationships. With anybody. Nothing personal. It's just that I have my life and I'm set in my ways and live the life I like to live. And that's really it. I don't do relationships with anybody."

He removed some hair from her face and lightly kissed her forehead. "Willow, I don't think I need to tell you that there's something between us. And you told me that rather odd story about two ghosts haunting you into writing a screenplay, and I didn't bat an eyelash because I believe you. My mother told me you have a lot of psychic abilities, so who am I to say you don't? I'd like to read the screenplay, however. After all, this will be my movie, so the screenplay's gotta be damned good."

Willow just shrugged her shoulders and stepped away from the computer. She'd been hard at work on the screenplay for months now, ever since she came to Los Angeles. She'd been working on it every day when Jackson went onto the set, to acting classes, or to his modeling gigs. Every day, Jackson left for somewhere, and when he was gone, Willow banged away on the screenplay.

Jackson raised an eyebrow. "You trust me?"

Willow grimaced. Of course, she trusted him. She trusted him implicitly. But, like everything else, she didn't want to admit how much she trusted him.

"Yes, I do."

"Okay. Then I'll go ahead and read the screenplay and give you some feedback. As you know, I know everything about the Fitzgeralds, both Scott and Zelda, so I think I can critique it pretty well. Is it done?"

"No. It's not," Willow said. "However, it has to be with Nancy by the end of this week because the script doctor has to get a hold of it and work his magic. As you know, the schedule is that everybody's going to get the screenplay a month from now. So, it's definitely in the home stretch."

So, for the next few hours, Jackson read Willow's screenplay for the movie he was working on. And after he read it, he found Willow, who was hanging out in the living room.

"It's really good," he said. "You've never written anything seriously?"

"No. I'm not a writer. I'm an alternative healer, a tarot reader, and a psychic. Not a writer."

He started to laugh. "Sorry to say, but I think you have a dim view of your own abilities. Because this screenplay is excellent. I think you have a knack. If I were you, after this movie, I'd try to write other historical biopic screenplays. You really seem to get to the heart of these characters, their essence, and you're able to draw it out with a lot of drama, and the beats are spot on. And you made it all very compelling. This movie is lucky to have you."

Willow put her hands to her cheeks and felt they were warm. Truth be told, she was extremely worried about the screenplay. Nancy Tallow had read what she'd been writing, and Willow had weekly meetings with her. Nancy never had much to say about the screenplay. But maybe that was a good thing because she didn't criticize it. She probably would've said something about it if she thought it was going in the wrong direction.

"Well, thanks," Willow said. "I figured that even if I screw the pooch on this one, it would turn out okay because the script doctor would get a hold of it and just turn it around inside out and upside down. But it sounds like maybe that's not going to be all that necessary."

"No," Jackson said. "I mean, I'm sure the script doctor will make a few tweaks here and there. But you've done a really good job. You're better than ghostwriting jobs. You should probably get your Writer's Guild card, so you're part of the union, and then make some contacts around the industry and make this your calling."

Willow knew why Jackson was so adamant about continuing her screenwriting job, such as it was. He wanted her to stay in Los Angeles. He knew she wouldn't be inspired to stay in that city if he didn't get her involved in the movie industry.

Willow rolled her eyes. "Here's the thing, Jackson. I really liked my life the way it was. And I plan on returning to it just as soon as the screenplay is finished."

"Suit yourself. I'm just saying you have a knack for this. Maybe you never knew before that you're an amazing writer, but you are."

And then he looked at her with his beautiful blue eyes that told her he really wanted to be with her, and he was breaking down her defenses, little by little. She didn't really believe him when he told her she was a good writer and had a knack. So, she didn't want to do what he asked her to: join the Writer's Guild and try to make a name for herself in Los Angeles writing screenplays.

That night, Willow's defenses went down completely. She finally allowed Jackson to persuade her to spend the night in his bed.

And then she left at 4 o'clock in the morning, while he was still sleeping. She was fleeing from her destiny, she knew. But, regardless, she wasn't going to stay in his apartment and face the fact that she finally gave in to the inescapable draw she had towards Jackson.

She was determined she wouldn't get involved with that man.

Chapter Eight

Hallie

Hallie was now in her new home in Venice Beach. She was excited about living in this place because it was roomy and modern. It was a house inspired by the architecture of Frank Lloyd Wright, all geometry and huge windows. Right outside her door was a canal, and houses were facing both sides of the canal. The great thing about this place was that there were basically two wings of the house, so it was almost like a duplex with two different units together.

In other words, the house was perfect for her and Conrad. Thus far, they were still really good friends and had not become romantic. And, now that they were living together, in a way, it was advisable they didn't get romantically involved. So it was nice that she had her own living space, complete with a living room, kitchen, den, and two bedrooms. Conrad also had his own little space, complete with his own kitchen, den, bedrooms, and living room.

It was Conrad's idea they get a house that was separated

in that way. He said they both needed their own lives and privacy, and Hallie had to agree with that. Conrad also needed space for his artwork, and that was what he filled his living quarters with – paintings and sculptures and photographs. He was in talks with Hallie's daughter Morgan because he was going to join her co-op. Morgan was excited about bringing him in because her co-op was looking for somebody immersed in the genres Conrad was working in. Morgan loved his Neo-Dada in his Neo-surreal works and also really admired his photographs.

Morgan was, surprisingly, excited about having her mother in the same city. Hallie worried Morgan would be upset about her being in the same city because Hallie just reflexively thought Morgan worried that Hallie would crimp her style. But, when Hallie called Morgan to tell her that she was going to be living in the Los Angeles area, Morgan was willing to welcome her with open arms.

"Mom, I'm really glad to hear that," Morgan had told her. "I want you to be a part of Zendaya's life." Zendaya was now six months old and was hitting her milestones well – she was laughing, babbling, sitting up on her own, and eating solid food. Hallie was delighted to be a part of the child's life.

And once she got settled into her home on Venice Beach, she immediately looked for a job. She finally got her integrative nutrition certification and had an interview with a wellness ranch in the Santa Monica Mountains. She got the interview because of her experience in life coaching and her certification in integrative nutrition, a modality of nutrition counseling that looks at people holistically. Hallie was now trained to look at the psychological reasons why people gain weight and help them overcome those mental blocks. And on the other end, she was well-versed in nutrition, too.

She got to the ranch, and the ranch director showed her around. The ranch was a series of small houses, along with a large central meeting area. Each house accommodated four clients and was equipped with four twin beds, a desk, and a bathroom. There wasn't a kitchen in any of the houses because everybody who came to stay at this ranch was provided their own meals in the large meeting house.

The scenic background of the ranch was just pure beauty. The ranch was dotted with an abundance of pepper and olive trees, flowers, and desert plants. It was situated on 10 acres of hiking trails, with majestic views of the Pacific Ocean below. *It's so peaceful up here*, Hallie was thinking. There was hardly any noise except the wind blowing through the trees.

"Now, if you get this job, you'll be working as a counselor," Annie McCormick, the ranch director, explained when Hallie got to the ranch for her interview. "This ranch accepts 24 people at one time. While the 24 people are here, they all come in together and leave together. So it's not like different people are constantly coming and going. Once you get one group of people, you'll work with them through the entire six-week program. Each of our counselors is assigned six people at a time, so we have four counselors, each of whom takes six people under their wings during the six-week program."

Hallie felt excited that she might have a chance to work on this beautiful ranch. She never thought she'd be able to get a job in a beautiful setting such as this one. It was just so peaceful, so zen.

Annie was a thin, wiry woman. She was around 5 feet tall and probably weighed about 100 pounds. But those 100 pounds were very compact, as Annie was a very muscular person – broad shoulders, small breasts, very taut and toned legs. She looked like a gymnast.

"I was a client about five years ago," Annie said. "I'd just gone through a divorce and gained around 100 pounds. I was eating my feelings. Feelings of inadequacy, low self-esteem, failure. I was convinced that nobody in the world could understand me because nobody in the world was going through the same thing I was." And she laughed a little. "Can you imagine? My husband had multiple affairs while we were married, and he had the nerve to ask me for a divorce after it all came out. I literally caught him in bed with another woman, and *he* was the one who asked *me* for a divorce."

Hallie looked at Annie and tried to imagine her with a weight problem, but she just couldn't. Annie looked like somebody who had been in shape her entire life.

"You had a weight issue?" Hallie asked her. "How did you overcome it?"

"It was mental. It's always mental. Before I was divorced, I wasn't in the shape I am now, but I didn't have a weight problem. I was small, but I didn't have a lot of muscle tone because my only exercise was walking a lot. And I stayed small throughout my marriage because I deprived myself of all kinds of food. I barely ate anything because I was so afraid, ironically, of my husband leaving me if I gained weight."

Boy, did that sound familiar. A controlling man, the fear of being alone, zero self-esteem. That described Hallie before she got her own divorce and moved to Nantucket to be with her friends.

"Let me guess," Hallie said to Annie. "Your husband probably had about 30 extra pounds himself, but he always got on you about eating and exercising because God forbid you gain a pound."

Annie smiled and winked at Hallie. "You got it. Except Timothy had 50 extra pounds, not 30. And whenever I'd gain 5 pounds or so, he'd make me get on the scale every day until I lost the weight, he'd make sure I didn't eat anything I wasn't supposed to, and he made me go to the gym every day. He said it was because my parents were very overweight, so I was prone to also be overweight. And that was true – my mother and father were both very heavy. But all during my marriage, I was 105 pounds. Which meant he started harassing me when I got to be 110 pounds."

Hallie shook her head. And she thought her ex-husband Nate was bad. Hallie had a very toxic relationship with Nate, mainly because they didn't speak very much and never liked each other. But he never tried to make her get on the scale or harass her when she gained weight, which she did over the course of their marriage. She gained around 20 pounds while married to Nate and got out of shape. She was in decent shape now because she did a lot of yoga and walking, and, after she got the all-clear from her cancer doctors, she started doing Pilates again.

Hallie and Annie walked along the hiking trails. It was a very hot day and extremely dry, but this was a very peaceful walk. There was a view of the Pacific Ocean from where they were, and Hallie was always awestruck when she saw the ocean from a high vantage point. It seemed to go on forever, and from their vantage point, with the sun hitting the water, it looked like millions of jewels were on the water's surface.

"So," Hallie asked as they walked along. "What happened after he divorced you?"

"I went a little crazy. I decided that because I was

married to the guy for 20 years and never got a Ding Dong, I'd get a box of Ding Dongs and just devour them. I love those. Do you know what I'm talking about when I say Ding Dong?"

Hallie knew. Oh, Hallie knew what she was talking about. Ding Dongs were one of her favorite snack foods – individually foil-wrapped chocolate cakes with frosting and a cream filling. They were sweet, soft, chocolatey and oh.so.-good. "Of course. I grew up eating Ding Dongs in the 70s. I haven't had one of those for a long time myself."

Annie started to laugh. "Well, the Ding Dongs were just the beginning. There were so many other foods I didn't have when I was married to Timothy, and I would have all of them. Doritos, frozen pizza, pizza in general, dessert. I started to crave things like brownie sundaes and fried chicken, and I told myself I earned these foods with the scars from my divorce. Six months after I started this junk food binge, I was 200 pounds and feeling like crap all the time. I no longer wanted to look in the mirror, but I still wanted to continue to binge."

"How did you get it together?" Hallie asked her.

"A girlfriend finally set me down," Annie explained. "I was pushing her and everybody away because I was so ashamed of my appearance and what I was becoming. I no longer called my friends back. I took away all the mirrors in my house. I just wanted to be in denial. The food was my friend. The food was something that never let me down. The food would never lecture me, cheat on me, harass me, or make me feel like I was 2 inches tall. But my best friend, Allison, finally showed up at my house and let herself in when I didn't answer the door. She's very wealthy and wanted to use some of that wealth to help me get my life together. So, she sent me here."

They were still walking on the trail. Hallie smelled the air, the smell of pine and eucalyptus and flowers. "Is this the trail the clients hike on?" Hallie asked her.

"It is. The clients hike five miles on this trail every single day."

Hallie was very interested in learning how this woman could get her life together in six weeks at the ranch. "How did you get things together when you were here?"

"Well, it's impossible to be up here in this environment and not do a lot of introspective work," she said. "There are no televisions, Wi-Fi, computers, or phones. The clients are allowed to read books - there's a library in the main hall, but the books in the library are positive and self-affirming. They're books about nutrition and self-help, along with memoirs of women who have walked through the fire and come through the other side, and novels dealing with positive feminist themes."

Halley noticed the wildlife around as they continued to walk along the trail. They passed by a small pond with ducks and geese lazily swimming along. Rabbits were hopping with their ears standing at attention, and hummingbirds were buzzing around the water. Hallie liked to be in nature, so this trail was speaking to her.

"So, how else did you get your life together when you came here?"

"Well, there were all the activities they put us through," Annie said. "It wasn't just the five-mile hike every day, but the other classes offered. I did boot camp, Pilates and yoga, and spinning classes almost every day, along with the hike. I went through intense nutritional counseling because I was starting to forget what healthy food tasted like. But most importantly of all, I went through a lot of group and individual counseling. The counselors here were able to drill down to my issues and find out why I was overeating. And they were able to give me mental strategies to stop overeating. And that really was the most important thing I got here. I was able to be mentally strong enough to keep the weight off. Which I did. I lost 105 lbs in the months after I came away from this retreat, and I've kept it off for the past five years. And I'm in better shape than I ever was before I started gaining weight."

They reached a certain point on the trail and started walking back. "So, after you lost all the weight, you decided to get a job here," Hallie said.

"Yes. Like you, I got an online degree in integrative nutrition, so I really learned how to speak to people where they are," Annie said. "People get out of shape and gain weight for various reasons. It's very easy to be out of shape and eat or drink everything you want. It's not only easy to live that way but, let's face it, it's one hell of a lot more fun to eat a brownie sundae whenever you want to, as opposed to turning it down every time you go out. It's not easy to adopt a healthy routine, and it's extremely difficult to maintain the healthy routine. If you don't have the right mindset, you're not going to keep a healthy lifestyle because it's just too hard to maintain over the long haul."

Hallie knew she would do a very good job if she got the position as a weight-loss counselor. She not only had the certification in integrative nutrition but also had gone through many of the same experiences other women had. The divorce, the weight gain, the depression and insomnia that came from living an unfulfilling life. She'd managed to overcome all that and lose 30 pounds and keep it off.

Hallie knew what Annie was saying, however. It was very difficult to resist the siren call of delicious junk food. It was immediate gratification when she'd open up a pint of

Ben & Jerry's and finish it in one go or when she'd get a meal of fried chicken, mashed potatoes and gravy, and cinnamon rolls. Food was a way of tapping into your pleasure centers and lighting them up. It took a lot of willpower not to indulge in all the foods she wanted to, just because when she was in the process of eating something delicious, there was no greater satisfaction.

She needed a strong mindset to overcome that, which was what counseling was about. She'd love to lead a group of six people, shepherd them through the six-week program, counsel them and get to the root of why they were eating themselves into an early grave. Turn all their negative mindsets around and show them how to break their destructive relationship with food.

Annie and Hallie arrived back at the ranch, and Hallie finally got a chance to see the main building, which served as a meeting hall, cafeteria, and a place to relax. The main hall resembled a ski Château, with a wall of windows that came to a point, 30-foot ceilings, wood paneling, an enormous stone fireplace in the middle of the room, and light that streamed through the windows. In the main area, where there were a series of couches and chairs arranged around the central fireplace, women were socializing with each other. They were laughing and chatting and seemed to really be bonding.

"Now, in this main hall, all the clients come in to have breakfast at 7 o'clock in the morning," Annie explained. "All the meals prepared for our clients are organic, plant-based, and delicious. Everybody is required to gather for breakfast. And then, after breakfast, everybody goes for their 5-mile hike. We try to complete the hike before it starts to get really warm. By the time they get back from the hike, it's lunchtime. And then, after lunch, there are group counseling sessions and group exercise classes. Spinning, yoga, Pilates, and boot camp. Six people at a time will go through group counseling. The others must take at least one group exercise class."

"What kind of activities do the clients do in the evenings?" Hallie asked.

"We play board games, and we also have another counseling session that isn't really a counseling session as much as it's a circle discussion of sorts," Annie said. "The counselors ask the clients a certain question, and they're free to answer the question in a group. If they don't feel like talking, they don't have to. It's just a way to draw everybody out. And before bedtime, the group goes through guided meditation."

Hallie didn't realize it, but this walk and talk and meet and greet with Annie was essentially her job interview. After Hallie asked Annie a few more questions about the program, Annie asked her why she thought she would be a good candidate to be a counselor there.

"Because I've been there," Hallie said. "I went through a divorce, a toxic marriage, and all the terrible feelings that go along. Feelings of failure, longing, and envy of other people who seemed to have it made. Loneliness, insomnia, and depression. And I got it all together, so I think I could also help other people get their lives together. It's what I do in my life coaching, helping people overcome mental blocks. And I learned all about the mental root of overeating through my integrative nutrition classes. It's really a matter of just drilling down into why people are overeating instead of just giving them the list of foods to eat and telling them to have at it. I mean, everybody knows that a diet of Doritos, Big Macs, ice cream sundaes and soda pop isn't good for you. Everybody knows you're supposed to eat fruits and vegetables, grains and lean protein, and unprocessed food.

So knowledge about what to eat is just one thing, but not the most important thing. The mental part is much more important, and I think I would do a great job of counseling people on this part."

Annie nodded her head. "You've overcome challenges and come out the other side. Have you had any setbacks along the way?"

"Yes. I got breast cancer, which threw me for a loop," Hallie said. "Before I got healthy – got out of my marriage, lost the weight, went to acupuncture to open my energy centers - I was in a very bad place emotionally and mentally. And I overcame that, but I found myself going to that dark place again after I was diagnosed with breast cancer. So, I had to tap into my reserves, the inner strength that carried me through my earlier challenges, so I could face this brand-new challenge of my breast cancer. And I did it. I was able to beat that cancer. So I think I know something about going from a negative and self-reinforcing mindset to a positive and self-reinforcing mindset and how important that is to live your best life. I think I could really help people here."

Annie smiled. "I like you, Hallie. I like your energy and think you'd make a good fit here. I'd like to go ahead and offer you the position of counselor. Basically, the counselor hours are from 8 to 5, seven days a week, although, of course, you'll have two days off every week. We have counselors here every day, but they work in shifts, so everybody has a chance to have some time off. What do you say?"

Hallie felt her heart leaping out of her chest and flying through the room. She couldn't believe she had got a job in this beautiful relaxing setting and that her job would entail working with people who wanted to improve their lives and were open to her counseling. She felt very fortunate to use her new certification in such a positive and life-affirming manner.

"Yes, I would love to take this position."

Annie gave her a spontaneous hug, and Hallie hugged her back. Hallie felt tears coming to her eyes as she lay her head on Annie's shoulder. Was this really happening? She was excited before when she was working with Willow at their spa on Nantucket. But, at that time, she was still working on getting her certification in integrative nutrition, so all she was doing at that spa was greeting customers and booking people in. When she started her life coaching business on the side, that was very fulfilling for her because she really enjoyed getting at the psychological roots of why people put up barriers to success. That was such a fulfilling job, her life coaching.

And now, she was going to be able to take all of her lived experiences, all of the knowledge she had gained through her integrative nutrition course, and all of the skills she had put to use in her life coaching business, and bring all of that experience to this new position of helping people become their best selves.

And she would do all of this in the most beautiful setting imaginable.

All of this, and she was living with Conrad, her wonderful British friend who made her laugh endlessly. Even if she and Conrad never hooked up romantically, she loved being with him. She felt very fortunate that he could come out to California with all of them.

After Hallie was offered the job and got in her car to drive the windy mountain roads down to the main road that would take her back to her Venice Beach house, she thought she was a lucky person indeed.

Chapter Nine

Ava

Ava met Elijah, her stepbrother, at a seafood restaurant in Venice Beach. The place served the best seafood in town, or so they said. It was an elegant place with white tablecloths, high ceilings, and an enormous window that looked out on the beach. Elijah managed to book a table on the deck, so they could hear the ocean rolling in and see all the lively beach happenings while they ate their meal.

Elijah was very handsome, with jet black curly hair, big brown eyes, heavy eyebrows, a very strong nose and jawline, and butterfly lips. He knew what she would look like because she had sent him a picture before she met him. So, when she went into the restaurant to meet him, he spotted her, greeted her, and showed her where he was sitting on the deck.

Ava sat down, feeling very out of sorts that she found her stepbrother so attractive. Well, then again, was he really her stepbrother? She didn't grow up with his family. She didn't know that his family was her family until just recently, and they didn't have any biological parents in common. The only thing that tied them together was the fact that his mother was married to her father. So, maybe Ava could fantasize about this guy just a little without feeling too embarrassed.

Elijah smiled and offered her some bread and a glass of wine from the bottle he had on the table. Ava gratefully took both things because she was hungry and ready to have a glass of wine. She was usually ready for a glass of wine, and she was nervous, so this time, she was *really* ready for that wine.

"So, I guess I'm finally meeting the woman who was so mysterious to me for so many years."

Ava cocked her head. She wasn't really aware that Elijah knew about her before this. "What do you mean?"

"Listen, I grew up in a family where there were a lot of secrets around," he explained. "So I always felt I had to keep on top of things because I never wanted to be left behind. You know, the last person to know something in the family, like the fact that I was born because my mom had an affair on my dad? Trust me, I had a way of finding out lots of things, like the fact that my dad had his own little secret. So I was curious about you, but I never told my parents I knew you existed. But, as you know, we have a lot in common. So, again, I'm really happy you called me."

Elijah had a little twinkle in his eyes, and Ava found that adorable. Esther had explained to Ava that in addition to his medical work, Elijah was a photographer, and his photographs were in collections. Ava wondered if his photographer's eye was sizing her up. If it was, she dearly hoped it wasn't found wanting.

"I'm glad I called you, too. Is it weird, a small world, that we happen to live in the same city?" Ava asked.

"Is Malibu a city?" Elijah asked. "I mean, technically it is because it's called the City of Malibu, but it only has a population of around 12,000, so I think the term 'city' is probably a stretch. But I know what you're saying. It's weird how life seems to work out. Anyhow, I know you wanted to meet with me for a reason, so go ahead. Ask any questions you want to."

Ava took a bite of her bread and a sip of her wine. The waitress came around and took their orders. Ava decided to order the swordfish with a side of Brussels sprouts and a side salad. Elijah ordered some crab cakes with a side of French fries and coleslaw. Ava realized her stomach was growling. She didn't know how hungry she was until she looked at the menu.

"Yes, of course," Ava said. "I wanted to learn as much information as possible about my dad and how it was to grow up with him. I got to know him when I was in my 40s, but I didn't know he was my dad at the time. I didn't know him when he was young. And I didn't know him on anything but a superficial level. By the way, your mother is a lovely person. She's a real joy."

Elijah nodded his head. "My mother is a fascinating person if you get to know her. She's a very modest person, so you might not know this from talking to her, but she ran with Truman Capote back in the day and was very friendly with his Swans."

"His Swans?" Ava asked.

"Yes. Truman Capote, back in the 50s and 60s, surrounded himself with elegant and beautiful society women who were also extremely intelligent and accomplished. My mother was not one of the Swans, at least not one of the inner circle of Swans, but she was friends with all of them, and my mother was so beautiful she could've been a Swan."

Ava had no clue that Esther was a part of such a rarefied community. Truman Capote was a very popular novelist in the early 60s, and he was the toast of the town after the publication of *Breakfast at Tiffany's* and *In Cold Blood*. Ava knew something had happened with his Swans, but she wasn't sure what. Something about him writing a book about them, and then they shut him out of their society.

And Esther was part of that group? Ava was impressed. She suddenly realized that she needed to talk to Esther much more because she was interested in hearing her stories. Esther was, of course, living across the country, but it would be almost worth it to Ava to fly back to New York and ask Esther about the whole Swan thing.

"How interesting," Ava said to Elijah. "I bet you really liked to hear your parents' stories."

Elijah took a deep breath and looked a little sad. "Yes. But you know, it's very important to ask your parents questions when you can. Because you never know when you're not going to get a chance to anymore. I found that out with my dad. I thought I had more time with him, but he had a heart attack just out of nowhere. I mean, it wasn't really out of nowhere because he was almost 90 when he died. But you're never really prepared. And there were so many questions I always wanted to ask him that I never did. So, if you have any parents alive, let my words be a lesson to you. Ask them while you can about the things you're interested in. You might be surprised by their answers."

Ava took a bite of her bread and a sip of her wine. "I know what you're saying. My father died when I was only five years old. Well, I mean the man who I thought was my father. Obviously, my real father, James, didn't die until just recently. But the man in my life for the first five years died before I could really get to know him. But my mom is still alive. And, up until recently, I was never close to her. But I am now. So, you're right. I really need to ask her any questions I can so that when she finally dies, there's nothing I didn't know about her that I wanted to know."

Ava was slightly surprised about some things she found out about her mom recently. Like the fact that her mother did LSD in her youth – twice. And the fact that she had a longtime lover who was a woman. Ava heard some of the stories of her mother's time at Harvard, but she needed to know more. When she talked to her mother again, she should think of herself as an investigative reporter trying to unearth stories.

Elijah smiled, a twinkle in his big brown eyes. "It's funny how you describe your biological father versus your father. You talk about your father as simply the man who was in your life for the first five years. But, you know, I'm sure he was more than that. I had the same problem when I discovered that my father wasn't James. How did I talk about the random guy who gave me life? How did I talk about the man who was raising me? I finally realized that the man who gave me his DNA was not my dad. He wasn't anybody to me. My father's name was James Bloch, and that's how I always looked at it. So, I'm not telling you what to do, but you should come to terms with it like I did."

Ava nodded her head. "You're right." The waitress came around and brought their food, and Elijah ordered another bottle of wine for the two.

Ava took a bite of her swordfish, which was delicious.

And then Elijah took a bite of his crab cake, cut a tiny piece off, and put it on Ava's plate to taste. Ava did the same for her swordfish.

"I really like this place," Ava said. "I'm going to have to remember it."

"How do you like California so far?" Elijah asked Ava.

"So far, it's very nice," Ava said. "I really love my new home. And I'm excited to be opening a winery with my sister. We just bought one. So far, there's not a tasting room at this winery, but we'll get the license for that. I don't know much about wine, but my sister does, and I have a lot of experience in running things, as I ran my own bed and breakfast in Nantucket."

"Yes, California is a very nice place to live," Elijah said. "You don't have the extreme weather you get in other parts of the country, and you don't have to face the extreme humidity of Florida or the extreme heat of Texas. And you also don't get the hurricanes you get in those two places, so you really have the nice weather year-round without a lot of the drawbacks you get in other places that have this kind of year-round weather. That's the reason why I'm living out here. I got tired of the New York winters."

"But your sisters still live in New York," Ava said. "And your mom. Do you miss them?"

Elijah shrugged her shoulders. "I guess. I'm not overly close with my sisters. I always felt so apart from them growing up. You know, my dad was different from their dad. And James treated me differently from them. He would've denied it to his dying day, and he probably did, but I noticed it."

This was what Ava was wondering about. "Differently, how?"

"It was subtle things," Elijah said. "My sisters got

birthday parties every year, and I didn't. My dad paid for my sisters' weddings, but he didn't pay for mine. Just things like that. I never really knew if the reason why I was treated a bit differently from them was because I was a guy and they were girls or because my father was a different father. And James felt that I didn't belong to him."

"How sad. It wasn't your fault."

"Oh, I know," Elijah said. "I've gone through a lot of therapy about all of it. You know, my biological father never acknowledged me. I even went to see him one day. I don't know what I was expecting when I went to see him. I guess I thought maybe he'd embrace me somehow. I didn't want to feel like he just rejected me, which he did. When I went to see him, he bluntly told me that I wasn't his son and nobody could prove I was. I wanted to tell him that there was a little thing called paternity testing that could prove it and that I could go to court to make a judge tell him that he was my dad, but I didn't do any of that. Neither James nor my mom knew that I was going to see my dad, so I just kind of left when my dad rejected me."

Ava took another bite of her swordfish. "Wow. You sound a lot like me. I struggled with the fact that my biological father, James, never acknowledged me while he lived, either. How did you deal with the rejection?"

"I pretended it didn't matter," Elijah said. "And it wouldn't have mattered if James would've treated me more like his son."

"I notice that you sometimes call him James, and other times you call him dad or father. Did you call him James at home?"

"No," he said. "My mom always wanted me to feel like I was part of the family, even though I didn't. So she always told me I had to call him dad at home. And I did that because I have a lot of respect for my mother. And I didn't want her to always be reminded of her mistake."

Ava took a deep breath. "What was James like at home?" That was what Ava was really craving. She wanted to know more stories about her own father.

"Well, he was a bit of a chameleon. An enigma. He had a terrible temper, and he drank a lot. I used to talk to my mom and tell her that she needed to leave him, but she never would because she loved him. But he also, most of the time, was a fun guy. He had a great wit. He used to go all out for Halloween, getting skeletons and huge spiders and inviting my sister's schoolmates over to bob for apples. He would have dry ice in a cauldron like he was a witch."

"Your sister's schoolmates? Not yours?"

He shook his head. "No. Don't get me wrong, I was popular in my prep school. I played sports, I was very friendly, I was in a band – I played guitar in an after-school rock band. I didn't have girls throwing their panties at me or nothing like that, but I did okay. But, no, when my dad invited people over, he never bothered to ask me who I wanted to have over. Just Rachel, Deborah and Val."

"Val," Ava said. "I'm so sorry about what happened to her." Val was murdered many years ago. She'd lived on Nantucket with her daughter, Jessica, and was killed by the husband of a woman who was at Jessica's fifth birthday party.

"Yeah," Elijah said with a sigh. "Me too. Val actually was nice to me, much nicer than Rachel and Deb, at any rate." He looked said. "Anyhow, my dad treated me very differently from them."

Ava was wondering about the wisdom of talking to Elijah about her father. To be truthful, James was coming off as a bit of a jerk in the eyes of Elijah. Then again, maybe James simply couldn't rein in his behavior. But she felt for poor Elijah. He was completely ignored by his biological father, and James, who raised him, didn't treat him fairly.

"Did you talk to your dad about why he treated you differently than your sisters?" Ava asked him while she took another sip of her wine.

"I did," Elijah said. "It was when he was a lot older, and I was too. I had kids of my own by this time. Two kids and I went out of my way to make sure they were treated the same. And, like I said, I had a lot of therapy about how my dad treated me. So, after I had kids of my own and I went to therapy, I realized how messed up the whole situation was between James and me. So I did confront him."

"And how did that go?"

Elijah shrugged. "He didn't really see what I was talking about. I tried to give him examples of when he didn't treat me like he treated my sisters, but he shut me out about it. He didn't want to confront his behavior, and he didn't want to talk about it. So, we got nowhere." He took a deep breath. "That was my one regret in life - he couldn't see my point of view. So I never really got closure on the whole matter. I had to go by what my mom told me, which was that James still had a lot of anger about the whole situation and was taking it out on me."

"But that's unfair," Ava said.

"Life is never supposed to be fair," Elijah said. "Anyhow, I got past it, in a way. I got a medical degree and threw myself into helping people in developing countries get medical care. That was the best way to get past my resentment for James and my biological father – charity work. Helping people who were so much less fortunate than me. It really puts everything into focus, going into villages with no clean water and barely any food. I started to realize that maybe my father didn't acknowledge me and James wasn't nice to me, but I had so many advantages in life. Everything I was worried about was first-world problems of the highest order. And I needed to just get over myself. So, I did."

Ava cocked her head and took a sip of her wine. "Yes, I can see how working with people who are desperately poor would really serve to put everything into perspective."

"It did," Elijah said. "I was over in equatorial Africa when I got the call from my mom that my dad had a heart attack and had died. And you know, I didn't go to his funeral. I told my mom I didn't want to go to his funeral because I never really thought of him as dad. She actually understood. She saw how he treated me compared to how he treated my sisters. But Rachel and Deborah didn't understand. I told them I couldn't leave my job to attend James' funeral because people needed me too much. They didn't believe me, and they've never really forgiven me. But that doesn't matter because I've never been close with them."

They finished their meal and got the bill. Elijah insisted on paying, even though Ava tried to tell him that was not necessary.

"Come on," Elijah said to Ava. "Let's go take a walk."

Elijah and Ava walked over to the beach. It was deserted, as it was dark, even though quite a few people were in the different bars and restaurants that lined the beach. As they walked along, Ava noticed a line of people with glowy headphones on their ears. They were the same people who were there before, men and women on spin bikes right there on the beach in the dark, following a silent instructor in the front.

"I should do that," Ava said, pointing to the people on

the spin bikes. "My friend Hallie is going to be working at a wellness retreat. She's really excited about it. She's going to be helping people overcome issues that are causing them to overeat or become unhealthy. She's probably like you, in a way, because she really enjoys helping people."

"Yeah, it really is a gratifying thing, helping people." Elijah took off his shoes, rolled up his pants, and then walked to the water. It lapped around his ankles and soaked the bottom of his pants, but he didn't seem to notice. "It's always a good thing, helping people who don't have as much as you. And it's also strangely gratifying to know that everybody has their own issues. And your issues are no bigger or smaller than anybody else's. But they're personal to you, so that makes them seem insurmountable. But then you get out in the world and talk to other people who really have problems, and you just realize that your problems amount to a hill of beans."

Ava realized that Elijah really had a good attitude about everything. And it sounded like Elijah's stint in equatorial Africa really helped him have this attitude.

Ava walked over to Elijah. "Yeah, I know what you're saying. We really do have first-world problems, don't we? I mean, we go to a restaurant that doesn't have a hostess, and we have to wait to get seated, and we have to wait to get served. And, you know, it's not the end of the world. We go on Yelp and act like the restaurant in question ran over our dog. But, in the end, it's so silly, the things we get mad at."

Elijah smiled and walked further down the beach. "So, tell me a bit more about yourself. Like I said, I've always been curious about you. I always wondered if you knew about us. If you knew that your father was James."

"No, I didn't know about James until just recently," Ava said. "My mom finally told me. And things blew up between my mom and me over that. I never got along with her and thought I'd never forgive her when she told me that. But I have forgiven her. We're actually really good, and my sister and I will bring her into the winery."

Elijah nodded his head as he continued to walk down the beach. They got to the part of the beach known as Muscle Beach because it had a bunch of exercise equipment on the sand. Rings, parallel bars, and other contraptions helped people work out on the beach. In the distance, not very far, the Ferris Wheel on the Santa Monica Pier was lit up. The middle of the Ferris Wheel had lights that turned into different things, like little hearts that rotated throughout the middle of the wheel.

Elijah and Ava walked over to the pier, and Elijah asked Ava if she wanted to get her portrait done by a street artist. The portrait artist was next to a magician with a large crowd around him as he did some tricks, and everybody clapped.

Ava smiled and sat down for the artist. Half an hour later, she had a well-done portrait finished. It was not a caricature but an actual portrait, and it was quite good. She looked at it and smiled, and Elijah looked at it and also smiled.

"Looks just like you," he said in a teasing manner.

They walked along the pier. It was the middle of summer, so quite a few people were walking about. Elijah and Ava wandered along, taking in all the sights. People were carrying lit-up balloons with cartoon characters inside. A musician played Disney songs, and people were dancing to the music. There were several different restaurants, most of them serving seafood. Among them was the Bubba Gump shrimp company, named after, of course, the Bubba Gump shrimp company in the movie *Forrest Gump*.

"Do you want to go into the Bubba Gump place?" Elijah asked Ava. "We could get a beer. I really like going in there, because I like to see all the memorabilia around the place. I'm a goof. *Forrest Gump* is one of my favorite movies."

Ava smiled and nodded her head. "Mine too. You know, after I saw the movie, I read the book."

Elijah nodded his head. "Me too. What a different experience, reading the book."

"Oh, I know," Ava said. "Personally, I found the book to be hilarious. Like I'd be reading it, and I'd be in the backseat of somebody's car, laughing so hard I was crying."

Elijah started to laugh. "I liked the part where he was blasted off into space and came down on that deserted island. It was also hilarious that Forrest was a physics genius and a chess wizard and that he met another chess wizard on the island who was also a native. It was just all so offbeat, that book."

"My favorite part was where he was a wrestler," Ava said. "Just how they described his wrestling moves cracked me up. But, you know, I loved the movie for completely different reasons from why I loved the book. I loved the book because it was so funny, but I loved the movie because it made me cry."

They decided to go ahead and go into the Bubba Gump place, and they both ordered a beer. And then they walked around the restaurant, looking at all the pictures and memorabilia on the walls. Ava smiled as she looked at all the pictures of Jenny, Forrest, and Lieutenant Dan.

They sat by the window and looked at the water below. There were still quite a few people on the beach and others in the water.

"You know, Ava, it's very strange," Elijah said. "I feel very comfortable with you. It's almost like we've known each other for a long time. I guess that's not so strange, considering we have something in common."

"Right. I guess we're kind of part of the same family, but not really."

Elijah chuckled. "Yeah, you might say that. At least, that's how I've always felt about my family. Like I was a part of the family, but not really. And you had the same experience, even if you didn't know it until recently."

They drank their beer and chatted comfortably like old friends. Ava was happy she got in touch with Elijah, even if he didn't tell her things about James that she wanted to hear. She only knew him as the kindly older gentleman who took her out for matzoh ball soup at Frankel's deli in New York City. He was always so sweet to her. And she adored him like a father, ironically. But Elijah had a different viewpoint on the man, and it wasn't a terribly flattering one.

Regardless, Ava felt good about getting in touch with Elijah and his mother, Esther, because it was like closing the loop for her. When she found out about her father, she didn't want to make waves, so she didn't want to contact Esther. Yet, Esther and her son, Elijah, welcomed her with open arms, which was heartening for Ava. Because their family was her family, too.

She even had two half-sisters, Rachel and Deborah. She was going to have to ask Esther if it was okay if she could get in touch with them because she had as much in common genetically with Rachel and Deborah as she had with Sarah, so she felt she should get to know the two women. Perhaps Esther would not object to her talking to them. If that was the case, she was going to contact them next.

But first, she wanted to talk to Esther about her past. It was very interesting to Ava that Esther was a society woman back in the 50s and ran with Truman Capote and his society women. She was interested in learning those stories. So, she was looking forward to talking to Esther again.

For now, she was happy she was getting to know the other side of her family. The side of her family that she didn't know existed until just recently.

Chapter Ten

Willow

Willow met with Nancy Tallow because she finally finished the Zelda Fitzgerald screenplay. Jackson had been calling her desperately since she spent the night with him in his bed, but she wasn't responding to his phone calls. And she never told Jackson where she was staying in Los Angeles, so he couldn't just show up at her door and try to make her talk to him.

Willow knew she wasn't treating Jackson fairly. But she was running from her destiny so hard that she didn't know who she was anymore. She hoped she could get the screenplay okayed by Nancy Tallow and then she could just leave. Go back to Nantucket, where her business was shuttered for the time being because Hallie was now out in Southern California. She didn't want Hallie to be out here, but what could she do? Hallie was only an employee of the business, even if she did put some investments into the new place. Hallie got her investments back, of course, but, at the moment, the Willow Tree Spa wasn't functioning, and it was June, her prime time. It was so frustrating for Willow, knowing she was losing so much money by being in California.

And the words "not functioning" described Willow herself. Being around Jackson was putting her off balance, to say the very least. She couldn't be around him without feeling the electricity between the two of them, electricity she wanted to avoid forever.

Willow learned from her mother Angela that men weren't to be trusted. Her own father, Jason, struggled with major depression his entire life, finally taking his life when Willow was only 10 years old. But that, alone, wouldn't have been enough for her to have sworn off relationships and men.

What was enough was the way Jason treated Angela. Her mother worked a full-time job, the same as her father, yet her mother was the one who did all the housework and child work while her father came home and had a beer and watched TV. And her father made her mother wait on him hand and foot. He seemed helpless, as if it was her duty to serve him his food on a silver platter while he sat and watched TV. One time, when her mother spiked a fever of 103°, she was still expected to get dinner on the table and do all the dishes. And her father had the nerve to still make her wait on him, as he was sitting in a chair and asking for a second piece of pie as if he didn't have two legs to get up and get it himself.

It was bad enough that her father treated her mother like a servant, if even that well. But, worse than that, he had affairs. Multiple affairs. Willow was only 10 years old when he took his life, but she was wise beyond her years, so she understood when her parents argued about her father sleeping with other women. They had fights about that right in front of the young Willow, thinking she didn't understand, but she understood every word. She knew her father was cheating on her mother, even though her mother was working around the clock between her full-time job as a nurse and all the housework and childcare she had to do.

Willow decided long ago that she would not get entrapped like her mother. Her mother, after her father killed himself, became a different person. But, unlike many women who go through such trauma, her mother became better. Happier. Freer. It was as if the death of her father liberated her mother. She was like the guards in the *Wizard of Oz* who were happy after the witch was killed because they were free.

Willow realized that her mother was like the *Wizard of Oz* guards when she saw the movie as an adult and realized that the guards probably suffered from something like Stockholm Syndrome. Because the *Wizard of Oz* guards were stuck in their situation and couldn't escape because the witch would've killed them, they adapted to the situation. They pretended they loved the witch and would do anything for her. But, once the witch was dead, it was time to celebrate.

Willow's mother probably also suffered from something like Stockholm Syndrome. She depended upon Willow's father for his financial contributions to the household. Maybe her mother was also afraid of leaving him because she didn't think she could survive alone. Whatever the reason, Willow's mother decided to stay with her father, so it probably took a Herculean effort to pretend every day that things were fine when they were anything but. Her mother did that for her, too. Her mother wanted Willow to think everything was fine in her marriage because she didn't want Willow to be afraid. Willow, of course, always knew better.

Whatever the reason why her mother stayed with her father, she did. Angela was unhappy because of it, and Willow always knew it. It was very telling that her mother never got into another relationship after her father died. Angela was a very attractive woman, and she was still quite young – only 45 years old because she had Willow when she was 20. And her mother was very in shape still. She rode her bike everywhere she went, and she was part of a biking group that went all over San Francisco, where Angela lived at the moment. Her mother did triathlons, and, to Willow's knowledge, her mother didn't eat carbs or drink alcohol at all.

And she was happy, Angela. Much happier than when her father was alive. Her mother didn't start competing in triathlons when her father was alive because her father didn't like her to have outside interests. He felt that anything she did outside the home was taking attention away from him, so her mother didn't work out when her father was alive. Her mother was quite out of shape when her father was alive, a complete 180° from where she was now – a fit, strong, confident woman who wasn't afraid of her shadow, unlike when Willow's father was alive.

Not only that, but her mother had a new profession, one that Willow's father would never have approved of. Angela was a psychic in the Tenderloin District of San Francisco and did very well for herself. Her mother admitted when Willow became an adult that she never liked nursing, but she did it because it was "respectable," and Jason was all about image. His having a wife who made a living as a psychic would've never gone over with him.

So, the lesson was, to Willow, that giving away your

power to a man was bad. Willow knew in her heart and in her head that Jackson wouldn't take away her power because he wasn't that kind of guy. He wasn't the same controlling man her father was, not by any stretch of the imagination. He was very laid-back. Regardless, the lessons her mother had imparted to her about men and relationships were deeply rooted, and they wouldn't be rooted out anytime soon.

"Okay, so the screenplay's done?" Nancy asked her after Willow met her in the coffeehouse. Willow had bothered to print out the screenplay at a local FedEx. It was over 100 pages long, so it wasn't cheap to print out.

"It's done. I printed it out so you can easily read it, but I also emailed you a copy. So, I guess I've done my part of the bargain. If you need me, I'll be across the country, on Nantucket, trying to salvage my business."

Nancy just nodded her head. "Okay. I'll read through it, make sure I approve it, and then submit it. Fingers crossed."

"Fingers crossed."

And then Willow left the coffee house and went back to her room.

But Jackson was waiting for her. He was sitting right in front of her room.

Willow had no idea how he managed to figure out where she was. But, somehow, he did.

And now she was going to have to confront him.

Chapter Eleven

Sarah

Sarah and Quinn were now settled into their new home on Venice Beach. It was a beautiful older home, built around 1920, rambling with nine bedrooms and three levels. One of the levels was considered to be the attic, but it was a finished attic, with the sloped ceilings that were typical of an attic room, but instead of exposed insulation and wood beams, it had a hardwood floor. Quinn saw that space, immediately fell in love with it, and declared that it would be her office, and if Sarah wanted to share the space, she could also put her office there.

The house's overall plan was typical of a house built in the early 20th century. That is, it felt a bit claustrophobic because every room was tiny, and everything was segmented off. There was a very small parlor at the front of the house, a small living room with a fireplace, a tiny kitchen, a small dining room, and every bedroom was tiny. Quinn immediately drew up plans to knock out walls so that everything was opened up. Quinn was a fan of the open concept, and she cleared everything with Sarah before she hired a crew to knock out the walls.

When everything was going to be done, the bottom part of the house, the part that was the living quarters, would seem so much bigger. Instead of segmented rooms, there would be just one big open space. And the kitchen would be greatly expanded, partially by taking out the parlor, which was unnecessary because there was so much other living space in the house. As for the bedrooms, they were all to be made much larger because they would be combined. There would be four large bedrooms and a smaller one that would be the guest bedroom.

So, Quinn and Sarah hired contractors and subcontractors after having gotten the proper permits from the city. The renovation would take six months, so Sarah and Quinn arranged to stay with Ava in her large Malibu beach house. Emerson and Julia, of course, were going to come along.

Ava, of course, welcomed them with open arms when they arrived. "It's going to be so much fun having all of you here," Ava said, giving everybody a hug. "I think all of you will love living right by the beach. I know you have your own home on one of the Venice canals, and it'll be beautiful when you're done. But, for now, all you need to do is pick a bedroom. The girls will have to share a room, but I'm sure that's okay with them."

Emerson and Julia were actually quite excited about the prospect of sharing a room. "I've never had a sister before," Emerson said. "And I know friends of mine who had sisters, and they usually had to share a room, and they loved it. Sometimes. Other times, they ended up wanting to kill each other. But I think Julia and me, we can get along just fine."

Julia agreed. "Emerson and I, we always get along." One

of the reasons for that was because Julia was so laid-back. She was the opposite of Emerson, who was opinionated, brash, hardheaded, and extremely stubborn. But, around Julia, she seemed to calm down a lot. Julia had that effect on people.

So, over the course of the weekend, everybody got settled into Ava's house while the Venice house was under construction. The five of them ended up on the large deck of Ava's home. The dogs - Kona, who was Quinn's Pug-Shepherd mix, and Bella, who was Sarah's Pitbull mix - joyfully ran on the beach, got into the water, and chased each other up and down the sand while Julia and Emerson stood on the sand and watched them to make sure they didn't get too far away.

"How is she doing?" Ava asked Sarah as Julia and Emerson stood on the beach, watching the dogs.

"She's doing okay," Sarah said. "She's in counseling. And her aunt lives right down the street, so there's that. But she doesn't talk a lot. At least not about Max. She's so inward, I don't really know what's going through her mind."

"Yeah, that's tough," Ava said. "I never really had to guess too much with my children because they have always been too forthcoming with their thoughts and feelings. Well, except for Jackson, but I always thought he probably just didn't let things bother him. Like water off a duck's back, that's how he dealt with problems in life. So, I'm sure he probably internalizes his issues, too. As for the other two, I definitely know what they are thinking at all times."

"Sarah's going to do great with Julia," Quinn said confidently. "She's doing all the right things, getting her counseling, and making sure she stays faithful to her religious studies. She said that her Judaism gives her a lot of comfort."

Sarah nodded. "I need to make sure she gets to the synagogue on Saturday mornings because she actually loves that. She loves the music, the prayers and the sense of community. We found a beautiful temple overlooking the Pacific Ocean. They even have Friday evening Shabbat services on the beach during the summer months. So, this Friday, that's where I'm going to be taking her. She's already met the rabbi, and they're very excited to welcome her into their congregation."

"Sounds like you got this," Ava said. "You just need to let me know what I need to do to help with Julia's transition. We know what she's talking about because we lost our father at such a young age. And we had our mother, but she was so cold and standoffish, it wasn't like she gave us much comfort. So we know about grieving."

"Yes," Sarah said. "But it wasn't exactly the same for you and me. We were still in our childhood home when our father died. So, it wasn't like we had to start a completely different life after dad died. We still had our neighborhood friends and we went to the same school. Everything was more or less normal for us. Our lives never made us feel like we didn't have roots. That's what Julia's going through. Everything is different for her. She has no roots anywhere at this point. She's moved from Washington DC to Nantucket and now here. I worry that she'll feel she doesn't fit in anywhere."

Just then, Julia and Emerson climbed the wooden stairs to the deck, the dogs following very close behind. The dogs were panting because they had been playing so hard, chasing each other and chasing toys into the surf and bringing them back. Neither dog was necessarily a water dog, as Kona was a cross between a pug and a shepherd, and Bella was a cross between a pit bull and something. It wasn't clear exactly what. Yet, both dogs seemed to have a ball in the surf.

The dogs got on the deck and lay on the hardwood floor, panting and exhausted.

"We're going to go inside," Emerson said. "We'll catch you guys when you come on in."

The two girls went inside, and Ava looked at Sarah. "You mentioned something about Friday night Shabbat services? What is that, exactly?"

"I'm not sure, but the website looks like it's basically singing, dancing, and services on the beach," Sarah explained. "On Friday night, starting at 7 o'clock. It looks like something that would be lively, and I think Julia would really enjoy it."

Ava nodded her head. "I wonder if my stepbrother, Elijah, would enjoy something like that. I should ask him. Anyhow, this is a good time for me to try to focus on the part of my family that is Jewish. I really would like to come with you to Friday evening services and maybe even come to the Saturday services at the synagogue."

Sarah thought that sounded like a really good idea. "Let's do it."

"Yes, let's," Ava said. "I'll call Elijah and ask him if he goes to that temple and see if he does the Friday night Shabbat thing, and if he doesn't, maybe he'd like to come and check it out."

Sarah nodded. "So, what is Elijah like?"

Ava shrugged her shoulders. "Not really sure. We only had the one dinner, and we walked on the beach. I think he's really attractive, but I'd never go there because it would be too weird. To say the very least." Then she started to laugh. "It would be like Marcia and Greg Brady getting together."

Sarah laughed. "It wouldn't be quite like that. After all, Marcia and Greg were living under the same roof, growing up together. You've never laid eyes on this guy until just recently, and you were never part of the fabric of his family. The only thing you have in common with the guy is his mother was married to your father. There's no blood relation. So, you should go for it if you think he's attractive."

Quinn thought that was pretty funny. "I'm with Ava. Sorry, but that just cuts too close to home. I know it happened on *Clueless*, but, in real life, it would just be too weird."

Sarah looked over at Hallie. "Well, Hallie, what say you? Do you think Ava should make a play for her stepbrother?"

"No," Hallie said with a shake of her head. "I'm with everybody else. I know Ava never grew up with the guy, but it does seem really incestuous. And that's too bad because he seemed like a cool guy, from what Ava told us."

Ava's cheeks were red. Sarah knew, realistically, Ava would never go for Elijah. But it was clear from her sister's expression that her sister wished she could. That was why Sarah told her she should go for it - she didn't want Ava to feel bad for being attracted to the guy. Realistically, Sarah thought it would be weird, too. But she would support Ava, no matter what she did.

"Anyhow, moving on," Ava said in a stern voice. "Okay, Hallie has some news. Hallie, go ahead."

Hallie nodded her head. "I have my first real job ever. Well, I know I was a business partner with Willow and worked there, but I didn't really do much there. I pretty much greeted people and made reservations, and offered them water. Oh, and I stocked the waiting room with really good magazines. I felt underutilized there. But I just found a job for real. A job helping people at a wellness retreat. I'm going to be a counselor for nutrition and the mental part of being healthy and losing weight."

Sarah raised her glass when Hallie told the ladies her news. "To Hallie, having her first real job. Good for you, Hallie. It sounds like something that's right up your alley, and I know you'll enjoy it. Tell us about the retreat."

Everybody else raised their glass and clinked it.

"Well, it's in the Santa Monica Mountains, and it's situated on acres and acres of land, so there's a beautiful hiking trail," Hallie explained. "And the people stay in little cabins, four to a room. The meeting room is beautiful, like a ski lodge. I'm really excited. I feel like I'm finally going to make something of my life," she said.

Sarah knew Hallie was always struggling just a little bit with self-esteem issues. She didn't know Hallie before Hallie came to Nantucket, but she had enough talks with Hallie to know that when Hallie was married to Nate, her self-esteem was exactly zero. At that time, she had nothing but failure in her life, or that was how she looked at it. She failed every job she had, mainly because those jobs weren't right for her, and she also felt that she failed as a mother. She overcame many negative feelings when she came out to Nantucket, mainly because she got away from her toxic husband and became a business partner for Willow.

However, Hallie never quite came into her own. She was busy studying for her integrative nutrition certificate while she was on the island, and she did some side work as a life coach, but Hallie really wasn't fulfilling her potential. And now, it sounded like she was going to. Sarah was thrilled for her.

Quinn put her arm around Hallie. "Sugar, it sounds like this job will be perfect for you. How excited are you? And when do you start?"

"This weekend, actually," Hallie said. "I'm going to be getting my schedule, and I'll have two days off a week, but they may not be the same two days every time. So, it's not necessarily going to be Saturday and Sunday as my days off. It might be Monday and Wednesday or something. But I'll only be working days, so yay for that. And that's a good thing because I want to have my evenings free for Conrad's showings. Conrad, as you know, joined Morgan's co-op, and Morgan is planning a lot of receptions at the gallery."

"And," Sarah said to Hallie. "The gallery is in the middle of gallery row, so, every second Thursday of the month, there's an art walk where people go from one gallery to another. Maybe you can make sure you're not working on first Thursdays, so you can be with Conrad and Morgan on those evenings. I've been to different art walks in the Monterey – Carmel areas, and they're a lot of fun. You get to meet the artists, drink wine and champagne, food trucks usually park along the streets so you can grab a taco or a lobster roll, and there's really a party atmosphere. I'd like to go to the next art walk, and I'd love to see Morgan's gallery."

Hallie smiled really big. "You know, I think this move will be really good for all of us, in the end. I'm so excited about working at the wellness retreat, and I'm so excited about Morgan's gallery and Conrad being a part of it. And you guys, Sarah and Ava, you're going to do a great job with that winery. Quinn, your daughter will be going to an amazing school for the arts, so she can get some intensive violin training. And Ava, you're close to Jackson. Everything seems to be coming together."

Everybody clinked their glasses.

"By the way," Sarah said to Ava. "Samantha is going to be coming out here too, isn't she?"

Ava nodded her head. "Yeah. Apparently, Grayson has a hit on his hands with his urban fantasy novel. He's gotten a lot of interest in it, including a producer who wants to make a movie of it and put it on Netflix. So, they're going to be moving closer to the action, and Samantha really wants to look into getting on a reality show here. She's always wanted to be on a cake decorating show, so her plan would be to come out here and work for a major bakery making wedding cakes and auditioning for cake decorating shows." Ava started laughing. "Hell, I wouldn't be surprised if Samantha tried to get on the *Real Housewives* show. Of course, she wouldn't qualify because she's not rich, she's not married, and she doesn't live in Beverly Hills, but I wouldn't be surprised if she tried."

Sarah started to laugh. "Your daughter, she's something else. What's going to be great is that you're going to have your son and your daughter out here. Now, get Charlotte out here."

Ava rolled her eyes. "I love my daughter Charlotte, but I think she's happy where she is. At least, I hope so."

The ladies listened to the surf rolling in and watched people swimming, surfing, and boogie boarding in the water. It was a very peaceful scene, and the sun was setting behind the hills.

It seemed like everything was coming together for everybody, Sarah thought. She was really excited about checking out the winery the next day.

Chapter Twelve

Willow

Willow crossed her arms in front of her when she saw Jackson sitting in front of her hotel door. "How did you find me?" she asked him.

"I talked to Nancy," he said in a very stern voice. "She told me where you were staying. So, I'm guessing that as smart as you are, the fact that you did not check into a different hotel means that you didn't really want to get away from me. Because if you checked into a different hotel and didn't tell Nancy where you were, I would never have found you."

Willow sighed. "Do me a favor. Pretend that you never found me, please. Just turn and walk away, and forget I ever came out here to help you. I've already completed my screenplay for your movie. I'm sure it's crap, but it won't be on me if it is. It's going to be on Nancy. I'm only the ghostwriter."

Jackson shook his head. "Seriously? When I talked to

Nancy, she told me that she read your screenplay and thinks it's dynamite. She thinks you have a talent for screenplay writing, and she even told me that you should get your Writers Guild card and start making contacts out here and writing screenplays on your own."

Willow felt flattered that Nancy liked her work, but she wasn't going to let on. "I don't believe you. I don't believe she said all that. Why would she say all that when, if I actually started writing screenplays on my own, I'd be her competition?"

"Because you wouldn't be her competition," Jackson said. "She doesn't write this kind of movie. That was the reason why she gave you this ghostwriting assignment. For some odd reason, her agents slapped her with this one. She prefers to write action-adventure and superhero movies. She's a proud geek, as she tells me. She thinks you should write many more of these biopic-type movies. These movies are very much in demand, there are always new ones coming out, and they're usually quite successful at the box office. You can make a living doing this, you know."

"I'll tell you what," Willow said. "If another ghost comes and haunts me and forces me into writing a screenplay on his or her life, I'll do it. Otherwise, I'm not interested. What I am interested in doing is going back to Nantucket and getting back to my life. That's all I'm interested in doing."

Jackson took her hand. It was as if he knew his effect on her and would break her down. "Listen, the other night was out of this world with you. I know you felt it too. I know you felt just how I felt when we were making love. I know you felt the connection. You can't lie to me. And you can't run from me. I've spent my whole life looking for this kind of connection with a woman, and I've never been able to find it. But I found it with you."

Willow bit her bottom lip. Yes, Jackson wasn't lying. She did feel all the feels when she was with him the other night. When he made love to her, it was just so right. She knew she was coming home to her soulmate when she was with him.

"Jackson, here's the thing," Willow said. "You just said you've been looking, your whole life, for a connection like you have with me. Well, I've been living my whole life avoiding the kind of connection I have with you. And I'm going to keep on avoiding it."

"Why? Why are you trying to avoid love?"

"Because," Willow said. "Listen, things are always so great in the beginning. Two people meet, they dig each other, and think they'll be together forever. But all that is before the honeymoon comes to a crashing end when the dirty dishes pile up in the sink, there are socks all over the floor, the kid has a fever and is screaming nonstop, the checks are bouncing, and someone is having an affair. Or both are drinking too much. Or maybe one of the parties has a mood disorder, and every so once in a while, they become Mr. or Mrs. Hyde. Or maybe they became Mr. or Mrs. Hyde on a regular basis. It's just easier to avoid any kind of entanglement."

Jackson hung his head a little. "Wow. You really are cynical."

"You say cynical," Willow said. "I say realistic. Tell me what I just said that was wrong in your book. You have this romantic notion that love conquers all, but my experience says it doesn't. If it did, the divorce rate would be zero. But it's not zero. It's over 50%, and it's safe to say that many marriages that don't end in divorce aren't happy, either."

Truth be told, a part of Willow knew that if she got together with Jackson, they'd be happy together. She didn't think Jackson would treat her like her father did her mother.

She didn't believe she'd be a servant for him, that he would cheat on her, or that he would put a pistol in his mouth at age 35 the way her father did.

Jackson nodded his head. "I'm not going to beg. I have more pride than that. I will tell you, and I know this will sound strange because we haven't been hanging out for that long, to say the least. But I'm head over heels, crazy in love with you. And I've been head over heels, crazy in love with you from the moment I met you. Do with that what you will. But I just wanted you to know I felt that way about you."

Just what Willow didn't want to hear. She felt the same way about him, of course. "Well, thank you for telling me that. And now, I have to get on my computer to book a flight back to Nantucket. So, I'm sure you have someplace to be."

Jackson looked defeated. "Okay. I said what I came here to say. You know where I am. You know where I live. Peace out."

And, at that, he left.

And Willow initially breathed a sigh of relief. She would carry on with her life just like she was before and forget she ever met Jackson.

Yet, at the same time, she was heartbroken. It needed to be done. She needed to slam the door in his face because he was getting way too close.

Then, an hour later, when she was packing her bags after having booked a flight into Boston, where she would take the puddle jumper over to Nantucket, she ran to the bathroom and threw up.

She stood up from the toilet and shook her head.

Yes, it was just that she suspected. After the night they spent together, she knew they had conceived a child. She knew that because she was sensitive to such things. However, she tried to talk herself out of the reality that she would have Jackson's baby.

But now, she knew she couldn't run from the truth.

She was going to have a baby, and it was Jackson's.

Chapter Thirteen

Hallie

The next evening after Hallie had wine over at the ladies' home, she was invited to Morgan's art gallery. It was in the middle of gallery row, a space in downtown Los Angeles with over 50 galleries in a few square blocks. Hallie got to Morgan's gallery, which she'd never visited before, and saw a reception was in full swing.

Of course! Conrad had mentioned that the gallery would have a reception to welcome him into the fold. Morgan had invited over 100 serious art collectors, and about 40 of them showed up and were drinking champagne and eating hors d'oeuvres.

Hallie admired the gallery. It was just exactly how she would've designed it if she was going to design a gallery. The ceilings were high, the brick was exposed on one wall, the other walls were white, and the floor was multicolored hardwood. People were walking around and admiring the art. Several of them were stopped right in front of Conrad's works and talking about buying them.

Morgan was nowhere to be seen, but Hallie soon saw her coming down the stairs. A loft with more artwork was above them, and Morgan apparently was in that loft when Hallie got there.

"Mom!" Morgan said excitedly as she made her way through the crowd. "What do you think about this gallery?"

"It's beautiful," Hallie said. "It's just how I pictured it."

Morgan nodded. "We're totally stoked about the space. We really lucked out, getting it. And I'm really excited about Conrad coming on board. He has brought a different perspective to our gallery, which I think will be very success-ful. We've already sold a couple of his paintings, and we have a serious bid on one of his sculptures. Where did you find him, by the way?"

"I met him through Charlotte, Ava's daughter," Hallie said. "You know, Conrad is not just an artist and photogra-pher but also a writer. He writes historical fiction based on real people. He likes to write novels based on artists in the past, like Picasso and Matisse and Soutine. In fact, I think the novel that Charlotte is working on is about Soutine and his experiences in Nazi-occupied France. I'd like to read that because I enjoy those books."

"Oh, I see," Morgan said. "He hired Charlotte to ghost-write a book? Wow. I knew the guy was talented, but I didn't realize he had his fingers in so many different pies. By the way, how is it living with him?"

Truth be told, Hallie and Conrad weren't interacting all that much, even though they lived together. Conrad was so busy getting his show together that evening that he was always gone. And when he was home, he was locked in his studio, which was the attic portion of their home, painting feverishly. Hallie would always bring him food and make sure he drank water while he was locked in his studio, but that was the only interaction she had with him. She knew better than to try to talk to him when he was in the zone. And he often was in the zone because he was a prolific artist.

"It's great living with him, I guess. I mean, I don't see him a whole lot."

Morgan smiled. "No, you probably don't see him a lot right now. He's been here at this gallery almost every night, helping us get his show together. And he told me he's been working like a fiend. But if you go into the other room, which is where his work is showing, you'll see that he's really in his element talking to the collectors. He's very charming, you know, mom. I wonder if you have an eye for him."

Hallie put her hands to her cheeks and felt that they were warm. "Goodness, no. I think I'm past all that, after what happened with your dad and everything."

Morgan laughed and waved her hand at Hallie dismissively. "Dad's a tool, and that's all there is to it. He's a bougie son of a bitch. You could do much better than him, and I've always thought that."

Hallie raised her brows at her daughter. "Bougie? What does that mean?"

"It means he acts like he's rich when he's not," Morgan said. "Haven't you ever noticed how he likes to flaunt his cars and his watches and the designer sunglasses he liked to wear at night because he wanted everybody to see he was wearing a pair of Chanels?" She shook her head. "It was embarrassing. I swear to God, he tried to cruise a couple of my friends by offering them rides in his BMW. And my friends were only 17 at the time, and he was 40."

Really? Hallie might have been naïve, but she never

thought Nate had been unfaithful to her. But maybe he was. Or maybe he was just flirting with Morgan's friends. Harmless flirting.

And then she realized she was making excuses for him. Again. Even if she didn't verbalize her thoughts, Hallie recognized them as being the reflexive way she always coped with Nate's somewhat embarrassing behavior. *Come on, Hallie, the guy was flirting with 17-year-olds when he was 40, friends of Morgan's no less. That was unforgivable behavior. Stop making excuses for him.*

"Morgan, that's disgusting," Hallie said to her daughter. "How come you never told me?"

Morgan took a deep breath. "Mom, I love you, but I knew anything I said to you about my dad would've fallen on deaf ears. I knew you would leave him one day, but only when you were good and ready. You weren't ready at that time. So, I just kept my mouth shut. I knew it wouldn't do any good, and you would just defend him or think I was making it up. You finally figured it out, so good for you. I'm only telling you about this because I want you to know that you could do much better than dad. And I don't know much about Conrad, but he's quite charming. You might give him a second look. Or, a first look."

Hallie took a sip of her champagne. "I'll think about it. In the meantime, he's my flatmate. That's what he calls himself. Flatmate. So I don't think he's looking to get involved with me, even if I wanted it."

Morgan nodded her head. "Okay. But, mom, I think you do want it. But I'll just leave you alone about it." Then Morgan put her arm around Hallie, and the two went up the stairs to the loft. Conrad was there, holding court in the middle of several collectors asking him about his work.

Hallie felt for him because she knew that Conrad, for all

his charm, actually hated glad-handing. He always felt he was asking for money when meeting the collectors and hated doing that. She knew he was uncomfortable, even though he didn't look that way. He also felt embarrassed when people told him how great he was. And, at the moment, that's exactly what was happening – the collectors were gushing over him and his work.

He finally made eye contact with her, excused himself, and walked over to her. "My flatmate, Hallie. Long time no see, huh, even though we live together. I'm chuffed to see you."

Hallie looked at his paintings on the wall and then eyed the group looking in their direction, obviously still wanting to talk to Conrad about his work. "I'm happy to see you, too," Hallie said. "But you better go over there and keep talking to those people because I can tell they're very interested in learning about your work."

Conrad smiled and bobbed up and down on his feet, his hands shoved into his pockets. "Yes, I have to put on my happy face and talk about my process and the meaning behind these paintings and sculptures." He rolled his eyes. "I hate all this. I wish I could just hang my paintings on the wall and not have to talk to anybody about any of it, but the world wants to talk to the artist. Anyhow, right, I need to get on with it."

At that, Conrad returned to the circle of people hanging on his every word. Hallie went back downstairs to look at the rest of the paintings in the gallery. The work of four different artists was being displayed that evening because that was how many artists were currently in Morgan's cooperative. They were all quite different in style.

One of the artists on display seemed to be more influenced by the Cubist movement, as the paintings were based upon figures composed of geometric shapes. The work was vaguely reminiscent of Picasso and other Cubist masters. Another artist whose work was displayed was evidently a pop artist. His paintings depicted iconic actresses and actors in different ways, such as Marilyn Monroe surrounded by graffiti or Audrey Hepburn with a multicolored face. Yet another artist on display painted pictures of beautiful women by the sea, along with a few abstract paintings of dancers and ballerinas.

And then there was Morgan's work. Hallie always knew her daughter was extremely talented. As she wandered around the gallery looking at Morgan's paintings, she appreciated just how talented Morgan really was. Morgan's work had a kind of mystical fantastical quality that was colorful, bright, and hopeful. At least, those words described her paintings. But Morgan was also a photographer. Her subjects were modern-day people who were extraordinary in some way, much like the work of the great photographer Diane Arbus.

Hallie felt warmth in her midsection as she looked at her daughter's artwork. She was just so damn proud of her daughter, she was bursting. She had no idea how she managed to get so lucky to have had a daughter like Morgan. Morgan was not just talented, driven and creative but also a very good person. Morgan had so much love for her family - her mother, her wife, Emma Claire, and their daughter Zendaya. Hallie was Morgan's mother, and that was continually a source of pride for her, who was a woman who often felt she didn't have anything to be proud of.

And the greatest thing for Hallie at that moment was the fact that Morgan was no longer the only thing Hallie could take pride in. Hallie had her own life now and was so looking forward to starting it. It wasn't like it was before, in

New York City, when Hallie desperately tried to hang onto Morgan's coat tails because those coat tails were the only thing sustaining her. No, now she had accomplishments of her own, so she could stand back and allow Morgan freedom to breathe and bask in her own limelight without worrying about sharing that limelight with her mother.

Morgan introduced Hallie to all the different artists that evening, seemingly thrilled to tell her fellow cooperative artists that she was Morgan's mother. Everybody was super friendly and excited about the new space, and they all seemed happy to meet her, too.

As Hallie drove home that evening, she felt on top of the world. It was the perfect evening for her. She got to see her daughter in her element, which was like a culmination of all the sacrifices Hallie had made for her daughter through the years. Her daughter was an amazing person, and Hallie finally allowed herself to understand that Morgan was the person she was because Hallie raised her to be that person.

And that was an accomplishment in itself.

Chapter Fourteen

Ava

Ava and Sarah went to see their new winery, and Ava was beyond thrilled about the place. At first, she was a little afraid of the drive up to this place. Driving up a mountain could definitely be a stressful experience. She was in the passenger seat, so she could see exactly how far up they were, and it gave her the sensation of vertigo to look down to the bottom of the ravine. There were guardrails throughout part of the drive, but only part and it was a little intimidating to look out the window and see just how destructive it would be if Sarah took a wrong turn some-how, maybe took a curve a little too fast. Ava imagined their SUV rolling over and over and over all the way down to the bottom if Sarah wasn't careful on her drive. And it didn't help that people were constantly tailgating.

I'm just going to have to get used to this drive, Ava thought. Once she got used to driving these winding roads up the mountain, it would hopefully be a piece of cake. As it was, though, the route to the winery was just slightly scary.

But they got to the winery, and the grounds were absolutely beautiful. There were groves and groves of olive trees that lined the property, and the view from so high up could not be beaten. There was a building right in the middle of the property that was a tasting room at one time, so it was turnkey.

The tasting room needed a little work because it hadn't been used as such for quite a while. The previous winery owners chose to distribute their wines and not have a proper tasting room. Yet, with the beautiful central building, a Spanish-style structure with stucco, arches and a Spanish tile roof, and the tables and chairs set up around the building, it was a perfect space to hold all kinds of events.

There were rows and rows of grapes as far as the eye could see. They weren't yet ready to harvest, as the harvesting season was from August to October, and it was only June. There were Chardonnay grapes, along with Merlot, Chablis, Zinfandel, Malbec and Sauvignon Gris.

Sarah walked along the grounds, a big smile on her face. "I can't believe this is happening," she said. "You have to pinch me and tell me I'm not dreaming. All this time, I've been dreaming about owning a winery. And now I'm going to do it with my sister. I just can't wait."

Ava was also quite excited about the prospect, but more than a little intimidated, as well. There was so much Ava had to learn about the winemaking process and the different kinds and varietals of wines. She never did learn a lot about wine. She knew what she liked, but it was always just a matter of personal taste with her. She never considered what wines go with what food, what wines are better as a dessert, what wines are best with appetizers, etc.

Sarah was going to give Ava an education about everything she needed to know, and Ava was looking forward to that. She felt that she would be starting from the bottom, however. That was unusual for her because she was so used to being competent with everything she did. Now, this was going to be something that she would have to learn from scratch, which was just a little bit intimidating.

"Yes, I can't wait, either," Ava said. "I hope to learn everything I need to."

Sarah and Ava were looking to open their winery completely by the first part of August. They would be processing their grapes by then and selling their wine immediately. Ava and Sarah had been working together to get a marketing plan. They wanted to appeal to the upscale clientele who might want to rent the place for any occasion.

The good thing was Samantha was soon going to be in California, and she would be working for a bakery making cakes. She already got a job with a major bakery in Los Angeles. Ava thought it would be a good idea for Samantha to get the word out about their winery to the people using her new bakery for weddings, reunions, and the like.

Ava couldn't wait for Samantha to get to California because she missed her sweet daughter. Samantha was always somebody who could brighten Ava's day. No matter what kind of problems Ava was going through at any given time, Samantha always made her feel better with her optimistic and cheerful attitude. And she always made Ava look at the bright side of life.

As Ava watched her sister walking around the vineyards, a huge smile on her face, she got even more excited about the prospect of owning this winery with Sarah. It seemed that this was a culmination of a lifelong dream for her sister. Sarah would finally be able to take all her years of wine study and put these years to good use. That made Ava feel really good.

That evening, Ava called Elijah. She wanted to see if he was going to the Shabbat on the Beach and if he was a part of the same synagogue Sarah would take Julia.

"Yes, Ava, I am a part of the Malibu Jewish Center and Synagogue," Elijah told her. "And I always take part in the Shabbat on the Beach."

"Great," Ava said. "My sister has a stepdaughter she's caring for. Her stepdaughter is Jewish, and they'll be a part of the same synagogue and taking part in Shabbat on the Beach. I thought I'd come along, too, because my father's family is Jewish and I feel like I should learn a bit more about the religion. So, I guess I'll be seeing you Friday evening."

Elijah chuckled. "Yes, I'll actually be looking forward to that. You can meet my kids."

Elijah was divorced. His wife, Abigail, lived across the country. Elijah had his two boys for the summer, both of whom were 15 years old. Elijah apparently was a bit of a late bloomer when it came to having a family, as he didn't have children with Abigail until he was 40. He explained to Ava that he was so busy with his career in his 20s and 30s that he just didn't have time to settle down. And then he met Abigail, married her, they had children, and then Abigail met somebody else and left him in the lurch.

The two boys, Levi and Caleb, were identical twins. Elijah said he could always tell them apart, but he was the only one who could. Not even Abigail could always tell them apart. Ava thought that was a bit odd because she always thought the mother would be able to tell her identical children apart. But, apparently, Abigail wasn't all that sharp when it came to that kind of thing.

"I'll really like that, meeting your boys."

"So, you're going to learn a bit more about your father's religion. That's admirable."

"Well, yes," Ava said. "I never really had a religion growing up. Any kind of religion. My mother is a proud atheist. Except she seems to be more agnostic these days because she lost the love of her life, and she's kind of finding faith. As for me, I've always somewhat felt it was missing, religion. I've always wanted to believe in something bigger than this world. And I've always thought the Jewish religion was beautiful."

"Just keep an open mind," Elijah said. "Even if you didn't have a religion growing up, you probably were exposed to Christianity. How could you not be? It's the dominant religion in America, so all the major holidays seem to be centered around Christian ideas. Easter, Christmas, and even Thanksgiving have always seemed like Christian holidays in this country. You need to understand that in the Jewish faith, our holidays more or less coincide with the Christian ones, because they're around the same time of the year. Passover is around your Easter. Hanukkah is around your Christmas. And then there are other high holy days - Rosh Hashanah, our new year, and Yom Kippur, our day of atonement."

Ava was familiar with the Jewish faith's high holy days and other holidays. She was always unclear exactly when Rosh Hashanah and Yom Kippur were, but she knew that Passover and Hanukkah were around the same time as Easter and Christmas. Ava knew that part of the reason Jewish and Christian holidays came at such similar times of the year was because both the Christian and Jewish faiths apparently wanted to celebrate the spring equinox and the winter solstice. It all went back to pagan days when early pagans had celebrations around these same times. Christianity simply co-opted the pagan holidays as their own because early Christians wanted to convert the pagans. One way to do that was to hold their celebrations at the same time as the pagans.

Ava wondered if it was the same thing in the Jewish religion. Did the early Hebrews know they were holding their holidays around the same time as the pagans? The Jewish religion was much older than Christianity, so Ava thought there was probably some other reason why Passover and Hanukkah coincided with the spring equinox and the summer solstice. That was one thing she was going to study. There was so much she didn't know. But she was looking forward to learning about the religion because she wanted to have something to grab onto in this world that made her feel a little bit less insignificant.

"Elijah," Ava said to her stepbrother. "I guess I'll see you this Friday evening on the beach. And I can't wait to meet Levi and Caleb."

"I'll see you, Ava," Elijah said.

Ava hung up with her stepbrother, and she couldn't help but think that she would be going into a new world.

And she was really looking forward to it.

Chapter Fifteen

Willow

Willow went to the drugstore to buy some pregnancy tests, even though she knew they weren't necessary. This was her destiny. She could try to run from it, but she certainly couldn't hide. Just like when Clara Bow and Zelda Fitzgerald haunted her into coming to California, this was one more thing compelling her to be with Jackson.

There was one thing she wasn't looking forward to: raising a child on her own. She knew in her heart that she was going to have a girl. And she also knew in her heart that Jackson would be beside her, raising the child together. She didn't think she'd be able to be a single mother, so she knew she'd need Jackson's help.

She closed her eyes as she peed on a stick. She looked at the pregnancy test, and there was no need to wait the five minutes or however long you're supposed to wait to get the results. No, the second she peed on the stick, the bright pink line became visible.

She was definitely knocked up. Damn! How could she let this happen? She knew better than to sleep with Jackson, yet, she did. It was only that one night, but apparently, one night was all it took.

Well, it was many times during that one night, so there was that to consider.

She took a deep breath and closed her eyes. She had to get her ducks in a row before she called Jackson. She would have to figure out exactly what she would do in California to make a living. Granted, she would get a pretty penny when she sold her spa out on Nantucket. So it wasn't like she would come to Los Angeles destitute. Regardless, she knew she didn't quite have the money to have a spot out there. There was too much competition, and it was too expensive to get a business going in the LA area.

Could she make a living being a screenwriter? She didn't want to admit it, but she really enjoyed writing the screenplay for Zelda Fitzgerald. She could get into the head of Zelda and Scott, find their essence, and bring it out on paper. It was a challenge, but it was an enjoyable one. And she never knew that she craved an outlet for her creativity. She already had one, in a way, with the paintings she created in her spare time. But the writing of the screenplay tapped into another part of her brain, and she really enjoyed it.

Perhaps that was the real reason why Zelda and Clara showed up and forced her into this situation. Perhaps they both knew what Willow didn't want to acknowledge - her destiny and fate were tied up with Jackson. And perhaps the screenwriting thing was all part of that − it was a dormant part of her psyche, the area that was an excellent writer. Nevertheless, it was a part of her psyche, and she accidentally discovered it.

And maybe, just maybe, this was what she was meant to do after all.

Willow picked up the phone and called Jackson. "Dude," Willow said to her soon-to-be husband? The very thought of that made her shudder. She never thought of herself as being anybody's wife. But that seemed to be where this was all going. "I need to talk to you."

Jackson seemed out of breath. "We're having a baby, aren't we?" Jackson asked excitedly.

How did he know? Willow thought. Then she realized that Jackson was on her wavelength, even if he didn't really know he was. That was why he had the flash of insight when he met her for the first time. That was why he was so bonded to her. When he told her he was head over heels in love with her, Willow knew that was because Jackson, on some level, realized his history with Willow. And, on this same level, the level that was deep within him, so deep that he could only access the feelings residing there by feeling them as opposed to knowing them, Jackson knew everything about Willow.

So, Willow shouldn't have been surprised that Jackson knew about the baby before Willow ever said a word. Yet, she was taken aback a little. But only a little.

"Yes," Willow said. "I'm knocked up. So, I need to meet you because we need to talk about this."

Jackson made a noise that sounded like he was giving a celebratory whoop!

Willow immediately felt annoyed that Jackson was apparently so happy about the situation. Didn't he feel out of sorts or apprehensive about having a kid with her? Why was he so on board with what was about to happen, considering they really just met, in this life, at least?

"I'll be right over," Jackson said.

Sure enough, in 10 minutes, Jackson was knocking on her door. Willow opened the door and saw Jackson on the other side, a dozen roses in his arms. That was a little weird because when did he have time to pick up roses? And then she realized Jackson was probably just waiting for her call. Just another data point for Willow that told her that she and Jackson were connected enough to know each other's moves.

"Come on in," Willow said to Jackson.

He walked in, picked her up, and swung her around the room. The second he did that, Willow started doubting that he knew her after all. Because she was not the kind of girl who liked to be picked up and swung around the room. It was almost as if Jackson had been watching too many jewelry commercials or romantic comedies or something. That had to be why he thought it was a good thing to do that.

"Willow, we're doing this. You and me, we're having a baby!"

Willow rolled her eyes. "Yes, I'm aware of this." And then she sighed. "Jackson, you're entirely too happy about this. You barely know me. Vice-versa. How do you know we'll get along, especially with a baby?"

Willow, truth be told, was very concerned about the whole aspect of child-rearing with Jackson. She envisioned herself being a very permissive mother. In other words, she was going to let the kid be who the kid was going to be without trying to guide the kid with a heavy hand.

Willow had met too many people who were screwed up because their parents had expectations that couldn't be met. Such as the boy who wanted to be a dancer, while the parents were determined he would be a doctor. Or the girl who came out to her parents that she's transgender, so she's really a boy, and the parents wouldn't accept that fact. Or the boy who had zero interest in math going head-to-head with the father who wanted him to be an engineer. Or the girl who had no interest in taking over the company coming up short with the parents who insisted she would.

And these were the people Willow knew over the years who acquiesced to the parents' demands and were extremely unhappy because of it. She also knew people who refused to give in to their parents, and that caused a rift between them. She knew several people who were gay, their parents were against them because of that, and they no longer talked to their parents. She also knew several people who married somebody their parents were against for no good reason, and they, too, didn't talk to their parents anymore. She knew a girl with parents who refused to pay for her schooling unless she studied law, like her father, and she wouldn't do that. She had to take out loans even though her father was very wealthy. She, too, no longer spoke with her father.

Willow was determined she was going to let the kid have agency. If the kid wanted to be a dancer, musician or writer, awesome. If the kid wanted to be a doctor, great. If the kid was LGBT, Willow would join PFLAG (Parents, Family and Friends of Lesbians and Gays) and would fly the rainbow flag. If the kid was transgender, Willow would do what she could to support any transition, including giving the kid gender-affirming hormonal therapy if necessary. Whatever the kid wanted, within reason, Willow was going to give it to him or her.

Of course, if the kid wanted to become a racist or a serial killer, Willow wouldn't support that. But Willow always believed in the concept of "live and let live," so as long as the kid didn't hurt another person, Willow would be down.

Would Jackson have the same ideas, or would he be one of those parents who would try to mold the kid a certain way? And that was just one concern Willow had. When two parents are trying to raise one child, there were a million and one landmines the parents might run into. For instance, with Zelda Fitzgerald, as Willow had been reading in her biographies, the father was a strict disciplinarian, and the mother wanted Zelda to have her freedom. So, the mother let Zelda sneak out the window to go to dances, and if the father ever found that out, there would be hell to pay.

Not to mention that Willow was still unsure about what she could do in Los Angeles. And she had to do something, that was for sure.

Jackson apparently wasn't worried about the same things Willow was. And, if he was, he wasn't letting on. He had a huge grin on his face. He moved to pick her up again, but she backed away.

"Willow, we'll be fine," he said. "We need to talk about how we want to raise this kid. I hope it's a girl, and she gets your abilities."

Her abilities. Yes, there was that. Apparently, the psychic thing was an inheritable trait, one that Willow got from her mother. When she wasn't cheerfully riding around San Francisco on a bike, her mother ran her psychic services out of a storefront in the Tenderloin District. She did quite well with it, from what Willow could tell. As well she should, because she wasn't a quack. She could tell the future and, like Willow, was in touch with the spirit world.

Willow wondered if her mother was ever forced into a situation like she was right now - getting stuck in Los Angeles, being haunted by ghosts who disappeared and now getting knocked up by her soul-mate who she didn't really know in this world. Willow often talked to her mother about the metaphysical things they both had to deal with, but, thus far, her mother never said anything about being haunted by ghosts that were as pushy as the ones who haunted Willow. So, maybe her mother escaped the pushy ghost thing.

Lucky her.

"Trust me, Jackson, you don't want this kid having psychic abilities," Willow said. "What I wouldn't give for the kid just to be normal. It's tough being in touch with the spirit world and knowing things you're not supposed to know. You don't know how tough it is."

Jackson just shook his head, the grin still on his face. "Whatever. I just want the kid to be as much like you as possible."

"Why not you? Why don't you want the kid to take after you?"

Jackson shrugged. "Oh, the last thing I want is for the kid to have acting in his or her bones. Because the acting bug just doesn't leave you alone. You have to sacrifice everything to the acting gods, and you need a strong spine to get through this world. This town chews you up and spits you out, no matter your level. It's a lot of pressure to do this for a living. And this is a town where dreams go to die."

"You're making it work," Willow said.

"After six years of being out here," Jackson said. "I didn't have a part before this, except for some cameos and walk-ons. And just because I got a major part in a major film opposite an A-list actress doesn't mean I'm on my way. This movie could flop and I could get the blame. If that happens, I'm right back to where I was before – auditioning and not getting a thing. Trust me, if I could force myself to be in a much more stable industry, I would. But this is the only thing I've ever wanted to do, so if I flame out, it will be bad. I literally don't have a Plan B."

Jackson had a point. As much as Willow was going to be hands-off with this kid, she hoped, for the kid's sake, the kid would want to do something stable and lucrative. If the kid was going to go into a creative field, she would support him or her 100%, but she knew it would be a difficult life if that was the case.

"Well, I appreciate you saying you want the kid to take after me, but I personally hope the kid takes after neither one of us," Willow said. "I want the kid to be well-adjusted, not screwed up, and hopefully interested in a field like medicine, law, engineering, or tech. Something that's in demand, and the kid can write his or her own ticket."

"Either way, as long as the kid has 10 fingers and 10 toes, I'll be good," Jackson said. "Yeah, it'll be great if the kid is a math whiz and becomes a professor at Harvard or something, but if the kid is a struggling artist, so be it. I won't tell him what to do. Or her."

Music to Willow's ears. "Really? You really don't want to force our kid to take advanced trigonometry if the kid only wants to be a writer?"

Jackson started to laugh. "Willow, I'm an actor. My mom never said a word to me about my career choice. She never once questioned why I wasn't going to college. She's always supported me. I'll do the same for our kid, no matter what. Do I want him or her to be an actor? Hell, no. But if the kid wants to be an actor and dancer on Broadway, I'll help him with a moving van. Or her."

Willow shook her head. She always needed to listen to her gut, even though her gut was off when it came to Jackson. She always had a hard time reading him, and he was the only one she ever had a hard time reading. The reason for that was because he was her soul-mate and had a veil around him when it came to her. It was counterintuitive – one would think that a person's soul-mate would be easy to read. But that wasn't true, at least in Willow's experience. She knew other psychics who were with their soul-mates, and they all said the same thing - they couldn't read their soul-mates at all.

But her gut told her that Jackson was going to be a fine partner and a fine coparent. They were going to be on the same page in raising the kid. She knew this.

"Okay," Willow said. "First things first. Here we are, imagining the kid 25 years from now, when, in reality, I need to get through the next eight months or so."

"*We* need to get through the next eight months or so," Jackson corrected her. "Willow, I know you've been on your own all this time. But you're now a part of a team. You and me against the world."

Willow didn't want to admit to Jackson that him saying that she was a part of her team was the second thing he said that was music to her ears.

The first thing he said that was music to her ears was that he would be hands-off with the kid's ambitions.

The second thing was that she was no longer alone.

She didn't want to admit to Jackson how much she loved him saying that she was no longer alone because she didn't want to admit to herself how much she needed him. In her quiet moments, when she was completely alone, before she went to bed, she knew she needed him. And before she officially met him, she always knew he was out there, and even then, she knew she needed him.

But, damn, that was tough for her to admit.

However, she knew she would have to do one thing before fully committing to Jackson in this scenario.

She would have to make a trip up to San Francisco to see her mother. She wanted her mother to tell her everything would be fine. That even if she and Jackson got married, it wouldn't end in disaster. Her mother could tell her that with her psychic abilities, but she could also just reassure Willow that things weren't as bad between her mother and her father as they seemed. And perhaps more importantly, she wanted her mother to give her advice on how to avoid such a situation as what happened in her parent's marriage.

"Jackson, I'm going to have to get away for a couple of days," Willow said. "I need to visit my mother in San Francisco. I hear what you're saying, and I think you're right — we can make a go of it. I just need to exorcise my demons. My mother, she didn't have a good relationship with my dad. And I need to get a little more information about all that. I was very young when my father took his own life. Before he did that, he was a bastard. That's the only model I have for marriage, and it's not a good one, to say the least. So, I just need to talk to her."

Jackson nodded his head. "I see. Go for it. I know you're not inviting me, and I'm not going to invite myself. But I just hope you get the answers you need, and when you come back, maybe we can plan our future."

"Sure. Anyhow, I'm going to get an airline ticket right now. Give me a ride to the airport?"

"You got it."

Chapter Sixteen

Ava

That Friday at 7 PM, Ava went with Sarah and Julia to the Shabbat on the Beach services. It being June, the sun was still high in the sky, even though it was Ava's understanding that Shabbat services were supposed to start at sundown.

Ava figured that if she was going to learn a little about Judaism, this would be a good place to start. The atmosphere was relaxed and the setting was beautiful, as it was right on the beach. Ava always loved being close to the water, as it calmed her down. So, the second she set foot on the sand, she could feel her heart rate start to decrease. This was good because she was nervous about seeing Elijah again.

Why she was nervous, she didn't know.

When she got to the beach, Elijah was already there, along with two boys who looked like younger versions of their father. They were identical, right down to their hair-styles. Like their father, they each had a strong nose, long

144

eyelashes, wild curly hair and bow-shaped lips. Unlike their father, their eyes were green, not brown, although there was brown in their eyes, just around the pupil. They were gangly and skinny, as 15-year-old boys tend to be.

Ava, Sarah and Julia sat next to Elijah and his boys and waited for the service to begin.

" Glad to see you, Ava," Elijah said. "And these are my boys, Caleb and Levi."

Two young boys shyly looked at Ava, and each boy politely offered his hand. Ava shook both of the boys' hands and smiled at them. "So nice to meet you both."

"Nice to meet you, too," Levi said. "Our dad says you're our grandfather's daughter."

Caleb appeared to snicker a bit, and he elbowed Levi in the ribs. "Nice," he teased Levi. "Just come right out with the whole 'you're our bastard aunt' line."

Ava had to laugh at that one. She couldn't argue with this boy's logic. After all, she *was* their bastard aunt. Or something like that, she wasn't sure what.

"Yes," Ava said. "I guess."

Elijah just shook his head. "Sorry about Caleb," he said. "I tell people he's on the spectrum because he just blurts stuff out, but he's not. He's just kind of a teenager. You know how they are."

Oh, yes. She knew all about teenagers, having raised three at the same time. "Not a problem," she said. "And this is Sarah, my sister, and her stepdaughter, Julia."

Everybody shook hands, and Caleb and Levi checked Julia out. Ava could tell that's what they were doing, even if they were pretending not to.

They chatted for a bit, and Elijah seemed to know everyone there. He was friendly with everyone sitting on low beach chairs, from the older women to the younger men.

He made the rounds, greeting people and joking around. Caleb and Levi got slightly impatient waiting for the services to begin, so they ran around, tossing a ball to each other and greeting other boys around their age who showed up and got in on the ball-tossing.

Finally, a man in a yarmulke and robe appeared, and everybody settled down. He greeted the congregation, held up his hands, and recited a prayer in Hebrew. Ava knew the prayer because she prepared for the services by memorizing the Shabbat prayer. Sarah did as well, but Sarah went a bit further and learned some of the songs that would be sung. Which meant that Sarah was already learning Hebrew.

Ava was impressed with how dedicated her sister was to Julia. Like Ava, Sarah grew up in a home without religion. Like Ava, Sarah always felt something was missing because of that. So Sarah started to learn about Judaism and liked what she was learning about it. She knew that to get a lot out of the services, she would have to learn the language. After all, much of the service was in Hebrew, as were the songs.

No doubt about it, Sarah was throwing herself into this entire thing. Sarah had also invited Mary, Julia's aunt. Mary was busy that evening but would be there next Friday.

The service was lively and, Ava thought, a lot of fun. There was a lot of singing, and even though it started with everybody sitting on the beach and singing along, everybody formed a circle and danced around at some point. Ava loved the music, and it sounded vaguely familiar to her ears. She was familiar with the folksong *Hava Nagila*, as most people were. She realized that many of the songs in the Shabbat service sounded somewhat like that particular song. But every song was lively and upbeat, with an amazing guitar player and singer.

She still felt out of place. She didn't quite know when to bow. She didn't know most of what was being sung. Much of the service was in English, but quite a bit of the service was in Hebrew, so Ava felt lost during a lot of service.

By the end of the service, Ava was having a great time dancing and watching everybody singing. At some point, a tambourine was passed around, and Ava gleefully shook it. Everybody was laughing and joyful because that was what a true religion was - it was a place to find joy, peace and happiness. And that's what the service was all about.

After the service, Ava, Sarah, Elijah and the kids went to grab a late bite at a restaurant on Venice Beach. It being a Friday night, the place was packed, but the group was able to find a spot outside on the deck. There were still quite a few people on the beach - surfers, a few swimmers, and lots of people gathering around fire rings.

Sarah, Ava, and Elijah all had a nice time that night. They stayed out until midnight. The kids wanted to go home earlier than that, so Mary, who was through with her event from earlier, came to pick the three up. They would all spend the night with her, so the adults could have some time to themselves.

Around midnight, it was time to go.

"Elijah, it's been so much fun hanging out with you tonight," Ava said. "I'm really happy I got in touch with you."

And she was. Elijah was much more comfortable around her that night than he was when they first met, so she was able to see his witty, somewhat goofy personality. He was intelligent and creative, and hilarious.

Ava was so happy to be part of his family.

Chapter Seventeen

Willow

Willow flew to see her mother. She didn't give her much warning, but, of course, she didn't need to. Her mother, being her mother, already knew Willow was on her way.

Willow got to the Tenderloin District of San Francisco and headed towards her mother's storefront. The Tenderloin District was one of the most crime-ridden in San Francisco. It wasn't gentrified, and the place was a haven for criminals, prostitutes, pimps, homeless people and drug dealers. It was also a place where there was a strong LGBT community, so the area was dotted with gay bars, along with theaters, art galleries and restaurants. There was also a vibrant Vietnamese community, so there were a lot of Vietnamese restaurants and quite a few Vietnamese people walking along the streets.

Willow absolutely loved this area.

Her mother's storefront had a large neon sign that announced she was a psychic. It was situated in an old brick building that was probably built right after the great earthquake and fire in 1906. Or perhaps even a bit before the earthquake and fire, although not many buildings survived those twin disasters - 80% of the city was destroyed over the course of three days as the fires raged and couldn't be controlled.

Her mother's space featured comfortable red couches, beaded curtains that separated the rooms, and smelled of candles and incense. Her mother made a lot of money with her tarot and past-life readings but also made major bank by selling various candles and crystals she'd personally blessed.

"Willow, dear, come here," her mother said when Willow walked in. Angela Killeen, Willow's mother, had long dark hair that grew past her rear-end, huge green eyes and a muscular and compact frame. She was a beautiful woman, and Willow always admired her for getting into the kind of shape she was in.

"Mom," Willow said. "I have news."

Her mother nodded her head. "I know. You're going to give me a grandchild, aren't you?"

Willow rolled her eyes. She couldn't ever give her mother a true surprise because Angela always knew ahead of time whatever Willow was up to. That was annoying, to say the very least.

"Yeah. Mom, can't you ever act surprised? Just once, to humor me, can you pretend you don't know what's going on?"

Her mother smiled the smile that Willow knew so well. That smile said, "yes, I can act surprised, but that would be insincere, so I won't." Angela shook her head. "Now, Willow, you know the score with me. You already knew I knew about the baby, so why do you set yourself up for disappointment? I'm sorry that you can't ever surprise or keep secrets from me, but that's how it is."

"I know, mom," Willow said. "But, yes, I have a bun in the oven."

Angela stood up and gave Willow a hug. "Oh, I'm so happy. How is Jackson taking the news?"

"Come on, mom, you know how Jackson is taking the news. You seem to know everything else, including that Jackson is the father."

Willow hadn't talked to her mother since she came to Los Angeles and had never even mentioned the name "Jackson" to her. So, her mother plucked Jackson's name out of the ether and, as usual, nailed it. And, since her mother intuited that there was a dude named Jackson on the scene and that he was the culprit in this whole disaster, her mother also had to know that Jackson was thrilled about the whole thing.

"I know, dear. But you just got on me about not pretending to know your news before you tell it, so I thought I'd throw you a bone. But he's very happy about the news, this much I know."

"Right." Willow took a deep breath. "So, you know everything."

"Well, not everything," Angela said. "Believe it or not, I don't know how you feel about it. I'm getting a lot of mixed messages about that. Sometimes you seem really happy. Other times you seem pissed. So, which is it? Are you happy or pissed about this?"

"Both," Willow said. "I'm happy because I want this kid, whoever he or she is."

"She," Angela said. "But go on."

"Mom, seriously? You can't even let me have that? I have to know right away what sex my kid will be?"

"Like you didn't know yourself," Angela said.

Willow sighed. "Yes, I had a feeling. But you just confirmed it, so thanks a lot. Man, I wish there could be at least a few mysteries in my life."

"Oh, boo hoo," Angela said. "You're going to be just thrilled to have a daughter. I think I even know what you're going to name her."

Willow was thinking of the name Naomi, which translated to "pleasant one," which Willow dearly hoped she would be. God forbid the kid was another version of Willow herself because she was a handful for her mother, and she knew it.

Willow crossed her arms. "Okay, go ahead. You know you want to."

"Naomi," Angela said triumphantly. "Or Natasha or Natalia. You're on the fence. Personally, I'd go with Natalia. I've always liked Christmas names."

Willow was astounded. While Naomi was the first name that came to mind, she'd also thought of the names Natasha and Natalia on the plane. And, now that her mother mentioned those names, they did seem to have a special ring.

Natalia, it probably was going to be.

"Yeah, Natalia does sound pretty," Willow said. "Everybody's going to think she's Russian if I name her that, but whatever."

Angela nodded her head. "Yes, I agree. It's a beautiful name. And it's a Christmas name, you know. It means 'born on Christmas Day,' and you know how much I've always loved that holiday."

Oh, Willow knew how much her mother loved Christmas. Her mother was the one who dressed up as Santa Claus when Willow was very young, even though Willow figured out when she was four that there was no Santa. Her mother was the one who held all the Christmas parties and decorated the house to honor the holiday. Willow could still smell the fresh pine in the trees that Angela would put up around Thanksgiving and wouldn't take down until long after New Year's.

All this was surprising for Willow, growing up, as her mother was a pagan. Nevertheless, Angela told Willow that Christmas, for her, was about fun, gifts and festivities. For Angela, it had nothing to do with the birth of Christ, who Angela didn't believe in. In fact, Angela did the Christmas thing more to honor the pagan holiday of Saturnalia, the holiday that the ancient Romans observed in December that lasted a week and entailed wreaths, singing, socializing, feasting and gift-giving, like today's Christmas holiday. Unlike Christmas, however, Saturnalia also featured copious gambling and human sacrifice during some of the earliest festivities.

Angela explained to Willow that she observed Christmas because that was what the dominant society observed, but, in her heart, she was honoring the ancient Roman gods that the earlier Saturnalia observers honored. Santa Claus was part of this ritual for Angela, just because Santa Claus was associated with gift-giving, and gift-giving was a major part of Saturnalia.

"Yeah, mom, I remember how much you love Christmas," Willow said. "Well, I remember how much you love Saturnalia, at any rate."

Angela nodded and smiled. "Yes, but I could never tell anybody I was honoring Saturn, the ancient god of agriculture, abundance and time. Everybody would've looked at me like I grew another head. It was always best to say I was honoring Christmas, just like everybody else was."

That was all because of her dad, Jason Killeen, Willow knew. Jason never had any special abilities, and he was a straight-arrow when it came to just about anything. While Angela and Jason were married, Angela never tapped into the energy of the universe, she didn't let on about her psychic powers and, most of all, she towed the societal line on just about everything. If Jason were still alive, Angela wouldn't have her psychic space, she wouldn't be giving tarot readings, and she still would honor Christmas instead of honoring Saturn, which she currently did. She no longer pretended to keep Christmas, for she told all her friends the truth about Saturnalia, and all her friends were fascinated by this "new" holiday.

Not only that, but Angela found other pagans through the Unitarian Universalist church she went to. These ladies honored Saturnalia the way it was supposed to be honored, except, of course, for the human sacrifice part. But the group partied for a solid week, giving gifts to one another and gathering at each other's houses to drink wine, sing songs and dance. They even went to the casinos during this period to honor that part of the Saturnalia celebration.

The Saturnalia gatherings always sounded like fun to Willow, and the ladies who gathered for the celebrations were a tight-knit group. Willow had met some of her mother's friends, who were cool women. Very laid-back, into nature, very generous, and most had at least a few psychic abilities. Willow always enjoyed their company. She was also happy that her mother no longer felt she needed to hide who she was. She wasn't celebrating Christmas. She was celebrating Saturnalia. Deal with it.

"So, mom, I guess Natalia it will be."

"Yes," her mother said, nodding her head with a big smile on her freckled face. "Okay, now I know you aren't here just to tell me about the baby. You want to make sure you and Jackson will get along in life. Right?"

"Right," Willow said, feeling it pointless to tell her mother a lie about why she was there. "I want to be sure."

Her mother cocked her head. "Now, Willow, I can do some cards for you, but you know the drill. Free will is always at work. I can try to see if it's meant to be with you guys, which I know it is. But I won't be able to tell you if you'll end up hating each other because of x, y or z. Que sera, sera."

Que sera sera. Willow always hated that saying and song. She wanted the future to become set in stone, something that she could look at and be certain that everything would go smoothly. But her mother was right - tarot readings would only go so far. They could give a good roadmap, but they wouldn't be able to tell Willow if she would end up trapped like her mother was, hating life and dreaming of something different.

"Mom," Willow said. "Here's the thing. I'm sure this isn't surprising to you, but Jackson is my soulmate. We've been together through many past lives. I'm sure a tarot reading will confirm that. That's not really why I'm here. I really need to talk to you about dad."

Angela nodded her head. "I always knew you'd want answers. What do you need to know?"

Willow took a deep breath. "Why did you marry him?"

Angela smiled. "I know what you want me to say. You want me to tell you I loved him at one time. That we met, the butterflies began, and the fireworks went off when we slept together. That we were enthralled in the heady first days of love and lust and got married because we believed that love would conquer all."

Willow shook her head. "No, I don't want to hear any of

that. Because if you tell me that, you're telling me that any great love can turn extremely sour. I'd rather hear that you saw red flags all over the place from the very beginning, but you ignored the red flags because you weren't in touch with your psychic abilities at that time. I want to hear that the signs were there all along."

The reason why Willow wanted her mother to tell her these things was simple - at the moment, Willow saw no red flags with Jackson. She was in love with Jackson, desperately so. The last thing she wanted was for her mother to tell her that she and Jason started out just like Willow and Jackson, and it all went very wrong. On the other hand, if Angela married Jason after seeing huge red flags, that would reassure Willow that Willow and Jackson wouldn't be going down the same path as Willow's parents.

"Well, dear, that's exactly what I'm going to tell you - there were huge red flags all along," Angela said. "Except there was a twist to this story."

"What kind of a twist?"

"Well, I knew I was destined to have you as a daughter," Angela said. "I dreamed of you my entire life. And, yes, I saw your face in my dreams when I was quite young. I didn't understand what I was seeing when I dreamed of you. At least at that time, I didn't understand. But I soon did."

That sounded understandable. Willow herself had similar visions and dreams that were about Natalia. She could see her face when she closed her eyes, that moment between drifting off to sleep and having her first dream of the night. Natalia would have bright red hair, pale skin, freckles, and green eyes. She was going to resemble the old literary character, Pippi Longstocking, when she was young. But when she got older, she would be beautiful, stunning even, with her bright red hair, creamy complexion and bright eyes.

"Go on," Willow said.

"Well, what can I say? To have you as a daughter, I had to have the right man," Angela explained. "And that makes sense to you, doesn't it? If I would've married a different man, I would've had a different child. Different genetics and all that. So, I knew when I met Jason that he was going to be the one who would bring me to you. That's all. To be honest with you, I couldn't care less about him, except I knew it was all meant to be."

Well, that was an interesting twist, indeed. Her mother recognized Jason as the one who would bring Willow about. So, Angela was saying that she made a sacrifice and married the wrong man just because she was determined to have the daughter she always saw in her dreams. And what a sacrifice it was, Willow thought. Her mother had to endure a jerk to get the daughter she knew she was fated to have.

"But, mom, you knew all along he was going to be an asshat?"

"Yes, Willow, I knew all along your father was going to be an asshat."

Willow took a deep breath. "Um, okay. So, you fell on your sword to get me as a child. Thanks, I guess."

Her mother started to laugh. "You're welcome. Anyhow, I don't think I need to tell you it was worth it. Every second I spent with that man was worth it because I got you out of the deal. You know you're going to do great things, don't you? You're destined for so much more than what you're doing now."

"Mom, I'm doing fine with my Nantucket spa."

Angela shook her head. "Actually, you're meant for more than that. I've always had a vision of you holding up some kind of award and making a speech. It's far in the future, but it's there. Right now, you own an alternative healing spa in a two-horse town. But you know you're hiding there. You've always been hiding there. For some odd reason, you've resisted your destiny. But you're not going to anymore. You're finally embracing it."

Somehow, as her mother spoke, Willow had the same flash of vision in her mind. She, too, could see herself winning an award for something. And she, too, could see herself giving an acceptance speech. It was all very hazy, as it was for her mother. And Willow had no idea why she would win an award.

"Mom, I just don't want to make a mistake. Don't get me wrong, I'm very happy about the baby. I'm just nervous about getting involved with Jackson, that's all."

Angela raised her eyebrows. "Well, dear, what is the alternative to what you're about to do? As I see it, either you give in to your destiny and you marry this Jackson, or you don't. No matter what, you're not going to be raising the kid alone, however. Either way you look at it, Jackson is one-half of the kid, and he's going to insist on half the say in raising the kid. What I'm trying to say is I know your prefer-ence is to raise your baby exactly how you see fit without anybody else's input, but that's not going to happen. Either way, Jackson will insist on being a hands-on dad."

Willow knew this without having her mother tell her that Jackson wouldn't be one of those absentee fathers, no matter what. Willow actually found herself wishing that were not the case. What she wouldn't give for Jackson to just willingly disappear from the kid's life, leaving Willow to raise Natalia on her own. But that wasn't going to happen, so Willow would have to buck up.

Angela put her hand on Willow's shoulder. "Willow,

you're just going to have to let go and let God. I know it's scary for you. You know how unhappy I was when I was married to your father. And I'm not going to try to say I wasn't unhappy. You're smarter than that. Just know that Jackson is not your father, you're not me, and if you have a good feeling about the guy, then go with that. Everybody's situation is different."

"But how can I avoid getting into the same trap you were in?"

"Well, that's a tricky one," Angela said. "But I can tell you that I went underground, in a way, when your father was alive. I denied every part of my soul when Jason was alive because if I hadn't, he would've caused our lives to be hell. He always had to have things his way. If he didn't, he went outer limits. I never wanted you to see your parents fight, so I avoided it by doing everything he said. I just wanted to make the peace."

"Mom," Willow said. "What if I do the same thing? What if I lose myself like you did because I want to make peace for my daughter, so I do everything Jackson says?"

"That's what I need to tell you," Angela said. "You can't possibly do that. With me, your father killed himself when you were quite young, and I could go on with my life and find myself again. I lost myself completely to a very controlling man. And, you know, I don't think I did you any favors in the long run. You knew I wasn't happy and your father was a jerk. There's just no other way of looking at it. I now know that I would've been better off keeping to my true nature, no matter how much my true nature would've made your father angry. Better for you to see me fighting back and fighting for myself than for you to see me weak and letting myself be led around by my nose."

"So, that's the answer?" Willow asked. "I have to make

sure I never deny my basic nature, and I live life how I want to, even if that causes problems in my marriage? Even if it causes massive fights that the kid needs to witness?"

"Yes, that's always the answer," Angela said. "Always, always, always. You always have to be you, Willow. Everything that makes you unique, you need to keep that. Because the second you deny who you are – a psychic, an artist, a writer, an intelligent, independent woman - you're on the road to hell, and you won't be doing your daughter any favors."

To Willow's surprise, she felt tears coming to her eyes. She was coming face-to-face with her biggest fear - she would lose who she was. She would deny everything about herself. She would fold herself completely into Jackson's life until she became somebody she didn't know. She would look in the mirror one day and not recognize the person staring back.

Willow finally nodded her head. "Thank you, mom. But I'm just afraid it's easier said than done. I just don't know how I'll avoid becoming one half of a unit instead of being 100% me."

"You'll figure it out," Angela said. "I have faith in you. You're a very strong-willed girl. You've always known your own mind, your own spirit. You need to stop fearing Jackson and just give in. That little baby is a sign that you're right where you need to be."

Willow raised her eyebrows. "Mom, I'm not where I need to be. I belong on Nantucket."

Angela rolled her eyes and shook her head. "No, you don't belong on Nantucket. What was I just telling you? You're not listening to me. I told you that you don't belong at that spa. You belong out here and are on the path you've been avoiding all this time. Willow, you're a writer. You've always been a writer. You just never knew it, but I always did."

So, what was her mom telling her? Clara Bow and Zelda Fitzgerald were haunting her because she ignored her destiny as a screenwriter? Willow always assumed that the two pushy ghosts were forcing her out to LA because she was turning her back on Jackson, and she had to face up to her feelings for him. But perhaps they were also haunting her because she was turning her back on her destiny, which seemed to be screenwriting.

"What do you mean, you always knew I was a writer?" Willow asked.

"Oh, you used to write little plays," Angela said. "You don't remember much about it now, but you wrote plays when you were only seven years old. You had me play different parts and your father too, and if we had friends over, they also had to play different parts."

Willow didn't remember any of that. "Oh. I was never aware I used to write stuff. How was I?"

"Very good," Angela said. "At only seven years old. You were like the writer's version of a little Mozart, sitting down to the piano at the age of four. You know, I've always thought of early abilities as being a vestige from a past life or two. Like brilliant masters like Mozart and Beethoven, who start playing the piano at age four or five and take to it like a duck to water, they were probably brilliant musicians in several previous lives. And you were probably a great writer in a past life because you were such a natural."

Willow furrowed her brow. "So, what happened? I started writing plays at age 7, and then, what? I just stopped?"

"Oh, you wrote plays for the next few years. You got

better and better at it, but then your father died, and you just stopped. I'm surprised you've forgotten all this."

Willow squinted, trying desperately to access the memory her mother was telling her about. She somewhat remembered it now that her mother talked about it. Her writing, long-hand, little plays. Her ordering her mother and father to play the parts she had written.

"So, when I stopped writing after dad died, what did you do? Did you encourage me to start writing again?"

Her mother looked a little guilty when Willow asked this question. "No, I'm afraid I didn't. I figured you would find your path again one day, but you didn't. You never even took a creative writing class in your high school. You just weren't interested in writing anymore. I have no idea why. But I knew it would find you again one day. And it has. You just wrote an amazing screenplay, and you will be recognized for it. Just wait."

"No, mom, I won't be recognized for this screenplay I wrote. I'm not the official writer. I'm only the ghostwriter."

"Willow, listen to me. You're going to get recognition for it. Just wait and see. At any rate, the writing found you again, and you have to listen to the call. Don't shut that door, like you've always been shutting that door against love and against your destiny as a writer."

Willow wanted to shut that door. She wanted her old life. It was safe. She was successful. She was never in danger of becoming something she never wanted, like what happened to her mother. She always believed she would own that spa until she was 100 years old and could no longer do tarot readings because she could no longer see the cards.

This new path was fraught with the unknown. She felt so out of sorts, which she had never felt about herself before. And becoming a screenwriter wasn't something she felt she could just do. Screenwriting, like any kind of creative field, was packed with competition. And there were so many established screenwriters out there that she would be up against. What if she failed?

If she failed, she failed. But her fear was that if she couldn't make a living in LA, she'd have to rely on Jackson's income to keep her afloat. And that was something she absolutely, positively, never wanted to do for two major reasons.

Number one, Jackson was in a volatile industry. He might have a hot hand right now, but who knows what will happen five years down the line? Unless your name is Brad Pitt or Leonardo DiCaprio, your future in the acting business will always be in doubt. Number two, she never wanted to rely on anybody for income. The second she became dependent on Jackson was the second she would have to go along with whatever he wanted. She would be that much closer to being controlled by him.

No, it could never work between her and Jackson unless she had her own money. She needed to believe that if anything happened and Jackson somehow became a controlling monster like her own father, she could get out. And the only way she'd have that kind of freedom would be if she had her own money.

Her mother, of course, read her mind. "You won't fail, Willow. You'll do fine if you keep on your path and ignore your brain telling you all these lies. Remember, you're going to get an award for something you're going to write. You're going to be at the top of your field. You just have to believe in yourself."

Willow, before this period, never thought self-confidence was a problem. But that was because she was established, and her life went smoothly. Since all this was so new, of course she was going to have doubts. She was human, wasn't she?

Willow finally just nodded her head. "Okay, mom, thanks for the pep talk."

"It's not a pep talk," Angela said. "A pep talk is made up of empty words that might or might not be true. You know I've never been one to blow smoke up your ass, Willow, and I won't start doing that now."

"Okay, whatever," Willow said. "Anyhow…" At that moment, the little front doorbell rang and several people came through the door. It was a group of four women, three of whom immediately were drawn to the crystals and candles. The other one looked at Angela nervously.

"My name is Chantel," she said to Angela. "And I have an appointment at 1."

"Come in, come in," Angela said to Chantel. "My daughter was just leaving. Come on back."

Chantel's three friends started to giggle. One of them made a joke about Miss Cleo, the famous psychic during the early 2000s who ended up under investigation by the FCC and the FTC.

Willow went over to Chantel, who was wringing her hands and looking very nervous. "Don't worry, Angela is the real deal. You're not wasting your money."

Chantel nodded, followed Angela to the tarot reading room, and Willow left.

She got out onto the street and felt somehow lighter. Her mother really was able to pinpoint her issues and put her onto a better path.

Maybe it was going to be great. Maybe it wasn't. But, come what may, she needed to make sure of one thing.

She had to be herself.

That was the only way it could possibly work.

She called Jackson when she got out on the street. "Hey," she said to him when he answered the phone. "I'm coming home."

"You are? And?"

"And, yeah. I think we should give it a go."

"I knew you would figure it out. Willow, things are going to be fine. You'll see."

Yes, I think you're right. At least, I dearly hope so.

Chapter Eighteen

Willow

A couple of days after Willow returned home and was reunited with Jackson, she had another meeting with Nancy. And that meeting set Willow's path much more firmly than it was before.

She met Nancy at their usual coffee house. Nancy was waiting for Willow that day with a coffee for her and a huge smile.

"I have great news!" Nancy told Willow. "I mean, really great news for you."

Willow raised an eyebrow and attempted to tame her queasy tummy. She hadn't eaten that morning because she felt so damned sick - how did her mother do it? How did any woman do this? And this was only the beginning. Willow had no idea, no clue, on why it was called morning sickness, when in reality, for her at least, it was all day sickness. It was night sickness, afternoon sickness and morning sickness.

In the meantime, Jackson was trying to force healthy food down Willow's gullet, when all she wanted to do was eat bland toast and oatmeal. The salads and Jackson's constant offers of tofu for protein - Willow was a vegan - just didn't seem appetizing to her. She tried to force down the food Jackson tried to force on her, but she couldn't for the most part, so she was losing weight instead of gaining it.

"What's the great news?" Willow asked. "And I have a doctor's appointment after this, so, I hate to nag you, but this meeting has to be quick."

Willow's first doctor's appointment was made by Jackson. Ava, Jackson's mother, still had no clue she and Jackson were to be parents. Jackson was dying to tell her, but Willow forbade it. She wanted to first get the all-clear from the doctor before telling anybody.

Won't Ava be surprised, Willow thought. After all, Ava didn't even know Willow and Jackson were even dating. Hell, Willow barely knew they were dating up until recently. She was so busy trying to avoid the whole thing she was in denial that their relationship was even romantic. Yet, it clearly was romantic, and then some. Willow's hormones were raging, and she was in love with the guy, so the two hadn't been able to keep their hands off each other for the past several days.

Yes, Ava and Ava's friends were going to end up gobsmacked by the news. Willow almost laughed when she imagined the look on everybody's face when she and Jackson dropped the bombshell on the group.

"Here's the great news," Nancy said. "I loved your screenplay so much that I told everybody the truth. I told George I didn't write a word of the screenplay, and he's really impressed."

"George" was George Kendrick, the A-List director for the Zelda Fitzgerald biopic. So, if he was impressed, that was saying a lot.

"Why did you come clean about the screenplay?" Willow asked.

"Because when I submitted the screenplay, George called me to rave about nailing it," Nancy explained. "He said it smelled of Oscar, that's how excited he was. And he told me he had more biopic projects for me to work on. Well, the second he said he wanted me for future projects, I had to tell him the truth, because the last thing, and I mean the very last thing, I want is to get a name for writing this kind of a screenplay. I don't want my agent getting more work for me like this in the future."

"Okay," Willow said. "What did you tell him?"

"I told him not to consider me for future biopics because I hate writing biopics. He told me he couldn't tell that by reading the screenplay, and I told him the truth. I had nothing to do with it."

Willow nodded her head. This all sounded promising, but she still didn't think she'd get a leg up in the screenwriting field. She was too new with no name. This could all be a fluke.

"Well, thanks for putting in a good word," Willow said.

"I just didn't put in a good word with George," Nancy said. "I sent the screenplay to my agent, and he's going to get in touch with you. He wants to represent you. Willow, my agent is with the CAA."

"The CAA?" Willow asked. The acronym sounded familiar, but she couldn't quite place it.

"Yes. The Creative Artists Agency. The top agency for screenwriters in Los Angeles. They represent the biggies who have won Oscars. You know, like Aaron Sorkin, the guy who won an Oscar for *The Social Network* and a ton of Emmies for *The West Wing.* Dudes like that."

"Oh," Willow said. "That sounds…"

"Willow, you don't seem all that impressed," Nancy said. "If you're represented by Bill Stone, who's my agent, you're pretty much guaranteed to get big jobs. He's one of the best. And he wants to represent you."

Willow wanted to feel impressed, but she didn't. The only thing she felt was nauseated again. "Excuse me," she said, and bolted out of her seat so she could run to the bathroom. Thank God this place had a bathroom, otherwise she would be in real trouble.

She went to the bathroom and worshiped the porcelain goddess. How long would she feel like this? At this rate, she wasn't going to ever complete another screenplay because she'd always be too busy puking her guts out.

She came back out and sat back down. "Sorry about that," Willow said. "Food poisoning or something."

Nancy nodded her head. "Ick. Been there. Anyhow, Bill is going to call you. He'll help you get your Writer's Guild card and everything. He told me he already has some projects he'd like you to consider."

"What kind of projects?"

"Well, he told me he has a project about Truman Capote and his swans that he's trying to find a screenwriter for."

Willow raised an eyebrow. That seemed familiar to her, for some reason. Didn't Jackson mention something about his mother knowing somebody who ran with those swans? Willow wondered about the concept of fate, and the intervention of the universe. Somebody, somewhere, put a bug into Bill's ear to tell him the Truman Capote swans thing was a good idea for a movie.

There were no coincidences. This was meant to be.

"Well, that's a great thing," Willow said. "I think I have a source for this, actually."

"You do? What kind of source?"

"Not sure. But I think my, uh, friend Jackson's mother knows somebody who knew the swans. Some 90-year-old woman in New York who knew those women."

Nancy's face lit up when Willow told her about her source. "See? That's perfect! You can write the screenplay and get some first-hand knowledge of the subject. That type of thing can really bring some color to the project." Nancy punched Willow lightly on the arm. "You're going to go far in this industry. I can feel it."

Willow, at that moment, couldn't feel anything but nauseated. "Thanks." She took a deep breath. "Well, Nancy, thanks for meeting me. Now, I have to see my doctor. I think I'm running late as it is."

Nancy looked a bit disappointed. "Sure," she said. "I really thought you would be over the moon about my news, though."

Willow smiled. "Nancy, I am. I'm just super sick right now. I literally can't think of anything but where the nearest toilet is. But I'm sure once I start feeling better, I'll be dancing the conga."

Nancy smiled, but the smile wasn't genuine, and Willow felt bad that she wasn't jumping up and down, as Nancy evidently expected she would be.

"Oh, no biggie," Nancy said. "But I don't think you appreciate just how big of an agent Bill is. He can open every door. Every screenwriter in this town would give their right arm to even get a meeting with the guy, and *he's* going to be calling *you*."

Willow closed her eyes, trying to imagine what Jackson would do in this situation. At that moment, she couldn't care less about this Bill Stone guy or about the Truman Capote screenplay that she might be assigned or about Nancy or about anything at all. As she told the crestfallen Nancy, the only thing she was thinking about was "where's the porcelain goddess?"

Yet, Nancy looked genuinely hurt by Willow's lack of excitement, so Willow was going to have to throw her a bone. So, she was going to think about her own acting skills. Jackson had taught her a few acting techniques on a lark one night when they were both drinking and Willow was in an unusually good mood, which was rare.

"Oh, Bill Stone?" Willow said when she opened her eyes. "Wait a second. I'm so sorry, when you said his name, it didn't register. But, oh my God, you're talking about *the* Bill Stone? The same dude who represented Aaron Sorkin?" Then she looked at the lights and tried to remember what Jackson told her about how he cried on command. Jackson told her about a thing called menthol tear sticks that actors use to cheat. The menthol sticks summon tears on cue. But Willow had none of these tear sticks.

So, she was going to have to go with Plan B. She had to think of a sad, emotional moment in her life and she had to do it fast. She was going to summon happy tears for this broad if it killed her.

In the end, she ended up crying for real. She simply thought about how overwhelming her life was about to be, with a new baby, a husband she barely knew in this life and the pressure of having to produce good screenwriting work in a dog-eat-dog town.

"Willow, are you crying? What's wrong?"

"Nothing's wrong," Willow said. "I'm just so happy, that's all. I've always dreamed of being a writer, and now my dream is coming true because of you! And Bill Jones! These are happy tears, the happiest tears in the entire world!"

Did she go overboard? Willow knew she was doing a crappy acting job. Jackson would laugh so hard at her right now if he saw her. She imagined the very worst acting performance she'd ever seen, and thought she probably went lower than that.

The worst acting performance she'd ever seen was on one of the *Gilligan's Island* movies that she managed to catch late one night when she couldn't sleep. Ginger Grant was played by somebody other than Tina Louise, the original Ginger. This actress looked identical to Tina Louise. However, this actress was so awful that she made Tina Louise look like Meryl Streep by comparison. Willow never imagined that *anybody* could make Tina Louise look good, but this chick managed it.

And Willow thought she was giving that bimbo actress a run for her money. Surely Nancy wouldn't fall for it. Surely, nobody would fall for it.

Yet, she did. Or she seemed to.

"Bill Stone," Nancy corrected her. "You said it right before. And he doesn't actually represent Aaron Sorkin, but his agency does." Then Nancy smiled, and, this time, the smile looked genuine. "I'm so happy you're so happy, Willow! I knew you would be thrilled when I told you the news." She clapped her hands together. "Well, yay! Bill says he's going to call you later on today. He wants to set up a meeting as soon as possible. I told him you'd be stoked, and I was so right! Anyhow, I can't wait to see your name credited on so many great movies in the future!"

Then Nancy impulsively got up and made Willow also stand up so the women could hug.

Willow nodded. Somehow, someway, her crappy acting job seemed to placate Nancy, for Nancy was now glowing.

Good. She seemed to make Nancy's day. Yay for her.

Now, where exactly is that toilet?

Heartfelt Friendships and New Beginnings

AINSLEY
KEATON

The
Beachfront
Christmas

A SCONSET BEACH NOVEL

vinci-books.com/beachfront-christmas

Family tensions, unexpected love, and miracles collide at Sconset Beach this Christmas.

As Sarah fights for custody of her stepdaughter, Quinn finds unexpected love with the vibrant Mia while mentoring Emerson and Julia's songwriting. Tensions reach a boiling point on Christmas Eve, forcing the gang to confront their past and forge new paths.

Turn the page for a free preview…

The Beachfront Christmas:
Chapter One

Samantha

Samantha Flynn, Ava's daughter, was still on Nantucket but that would soon change. Her boyfriend Grayson had been working on a fantasy novel for the better part of three years. It was a doorstopper of a book, and he self-published it. He told Samantha that plenty of fantasy authors were self-publishing their books and making major money on them.

Grayson sent his book to a whole crew of beta readers, and beta readers were all unanimous about the book - Grayson wrote a winner. Beta readers were people who read and review books before they were published. These readers were telling him that it was very good.

And then Grayson published the book, ran a bunch of ads for it, and hit the market just right. He got really lucky and somehow, the book ended up on the Kindle belonging to Cecelia Knox, a Netflix executive who was very interested in creating a limited series out of the book. Apparently, Cecelia was sick one weekend and had nothing to do but read. She came across Grayson's book that weekend and loved it.

It was a lucky break, for sure. The upshot was that Grayson wanted to move to Los Angeles to be closer to the action. He had meetings lined up with various Netflix executives, and, hopefully, this book would be picked up for a limited-run series. If it was, Grayson imagined he would be involved in many more meetings. So, Grayson decided that he and Samantha should move to Los Angeles.

At first, Samantha didn't like the idea. She'd made a name for herself there on Nantucket as the creator of beautiful, creative, and original cakes of all types. She really enjoyed making wedding cakes, but she soon found herself making cakes for other occasions as well. Anniversaries, birthdays, gender reveals, wedding and baby showers – Samantha cheerfully made cakes for all these occasions and more. She was getting very good at it, and she was very much in demand. Javier, her boss and the man who owned the bakery where she worked, loved her work and had given her several raises, promotions and bonuses because he wanted to keep her happy.

And she *was* happy at the bakery. Very happy. She felt that if she left Javier, she would be doing him dirty. He had been hinting around to her about making her a partner in the bakery, which would really increase her yearly salary.

But Grayson was adamant that he wanted to move to Los Angeles. He pretty much told Samantha he was going to move to the West Coast whether she came or not. This left her with no choice but to say yes to him. There was just no way that Samantha was going to let her best friend and boyfriend, Grayson, live across the country from her. So, she agreed to move with him.

Some headhunters from Los Angeles had contacted

Samantha, so she called back the headhunters and agreed to come out to Los Angeles for the best job they could find for her, and that was how she got a new job with one of the top wedding bakeries and catering firms in Los Angeles, called the Sweet Fantasy Bakery. This was a bakery that often catered to celebrity events, so Samantha was very much looking forward to meeting some television and movie actors, actresses, and directors. Maybe even meet a reality star or two.

In the meantime, it was time to pack, and that thought overwhelmed her. Oh, she hated moving. But the thing of it was, the place where she and Grayson were currently staying was tiny. It was basically the mother-in-law quarters of a gay couple. It was designed just like the large house but was about 1/3 of the size of the large house. Because of that, she and Grayson didn't accumulate too much over the years.

Nevertheless, she looked around her house and despaired. There was a part of her that was desperate for some kind of stability in her life. Her life before coming to Nantucket was so unstable that Samantha often feared dying quite young. She always took a lot of chances in her life, chances that were not exactly advisable. Whether she was meeting a random guy across the country after only talking to him on the Internet, or walking home from the bar at 3 o'clock in the morning through sketchy neighborhoods, Samantha lived life on the edge. And she was so ready to change it that she was thrilled to be living on tiny little Nantucket, where she didn't think she could get into much trouble.

Of course, Samantha being Samantha, she did get into trouble when she first got to Nantucket. She almost drowned in the ocean and was saved by a dude named

Adrian, who was wealthy and a bit of a douche. No, he wasn't a bit of a douche, but a full-on one. Samantha was over him from the first date, and then she dated another rich guy, and finally ended up with Grayson, her best friend of six years who had loved her all along.

And the stability of the tiny island was a great relief for Samantha. She no longer had to worry about walking through sketchy neighborhoods and looking over her shoulder for some bad guy to pop out and attack her. Because she found love with Grayson, she wasn't looking for randos on the internet anymore. In short, Samantha no longer feared she would be dead by the age of 30.

Now, she was moving to another big city, and she wondered if it was going to be a step backward for her. She worried she would fall back into some of her old bad habits when she moved out to Los Angeles.

But she was excited about being out there because she wanted to be closer to her family. Both her mother and her aunt were living out there, and Samantha had just gotten to know her Aunt Sarah and she really loved her. And now her mother and her Aunt Sarah were opening up a winery together, and it would be perfect if Samantha's new bakery, the Sweet Fantasy bakery, could partner with Sarah's new winery.

After all, the Sweet Fantasy bakery not only supplied wedding cakes for different functions but also catered events. These events, of course, needed lots and lots of alcohol, especially wine. So Sarah talked to the bakery about the possibility they would supply cakes to functions held at the winery, and they would use wines from the winery for the other functions the bakery catered to.

Her new boss, Kayla Brentwood, seemed to love Samantha. The two had exchanged emails and had spoken to one another on Zoom several times. And they seemed to really click with one another. Their personalities meshed really well. Kayla wasn't too much older than Samantha - she was only 30 years old, and Samantha had just turned 25. Samantha was very bubbly and very unfiltered in her speech, so she and Kayla chatted over Zoom about everything under the sun. They talked about movies they'd seen, series they loved, reality shows they were digging, and music.

It was ostensibly a job interview, but Samantha forgot that the purpose of the Zoom call was that Kayla was looking to hire a new cake decorator. She started to feel like she was chatting with a brand-new friend. By the time the Zoom call was through, about an hour after it began, Kayla formally offered Samantha the job with the Sweet Fantasy Bakery, and Samantha gleefully accepted.

Then it was a matter of talking to Javier, who didn't take the news well. "Samantha, you can't do this," he pleaded. "It's summertime. This is my biggest time of year. I have weddings lined up all summer long, and I need you." He looked like he wanted to cry. Samantha felt badly for him but at the same time, she couldn't arrange her entire life around him.

"I'm really sorry. But, like I said, Grayson's moving to Los Angeles, and I'm going with him. I'm sorry. Really I am, but I have no choice."

Javier shook his head. "I made you. If it weren't for me, you would be nobody. This is how you repay me?"

Samantha took a deep breath. Javier was not at all being fair. After all, the only reason why Samantha got the gig that made her, which was a society wedding for which she absolutely nailed the cake, was because the previous cake maker had quit with no notice at all. And, at first,

Javier did not want Samantha to work on that cake. In fact, he made phone calls all that day trying to find somebody, anybody, who would be able to do it on short notice. Samantha stepped up to the plate and saved Javier's bacon, but it wasn't Javier's choice at all. In fact, if it was up to Javier, the previous baker, whose name was Cynthia, would still be making the wedding cakes for the bakery. Javier just wasn't going to give Samantha a chance to do anything creative if not for the fact that the emergency forced his hand.

"Javier, again, I'm sorry," Samantha said. "But I seem to remember you making phone calls to everybody and their brother and sister when Cynthia quit that day because you didn't want me to work on that cake at all. So, maybe you made me, but it wasn't your choice. It was Cynthia who irresponsibly left you without any notice at all. I'm giving you two weeks' notice, unlike her. Now, there's nothing you can do to change my mind about leaving for Los Angeles. So I suggest you don't even try."

Samantha wasn't usually so stern with her words, but Javier really pissed her off. He was trying to guilt trip her into staying, and that really made Samantha see red. If there is one thing she hated, it was a manipulative person. And that's exactly what Javier was trying to do. Manipulate her.

Javier knew he was in the wrong because he knew what Samantha was saying was right. He didn't want her to work the Lawrence wedding. He even referred to her as an amateur. Now, he needed her, and he was going to make life difficult for her by making her feel guilty. Samantha wasn't going to be having that.

Javier shook his head and started talking rapidly in Spanish. Samantha didn't know a word of Spanish, so she had no idea what he was saying but she was sure she heard at least a few Spanish curse words.

"Okay, just go, go. You don't even have to give me two weeks' notice. In fact, I don't want to see your face anymore, so go."

Samantha just rolled her eyes. Talk about cutting off your nose to spite your face, she thought. There was a wedding that was coming up that weekend, and Samantha had planned to make the cake for that wedding. But, since Javier was essentially firing by telling her she couldn't put in notice, he was going to have to find somebody on short notice again. Instead of doing things professionally by allowing Samantha to put in notice and make the cake for that wedding, he was letting his temper get the best of him. And he was going to pay for it because Samantha was going to take him up on his offer to just leave.

After all, Grayson was already out in Los Angeles, waiting for her to move out there as well. Grayson had a bunch of meetings set up, so he couldn't wait around for her to get out from under her job. He had to get out there, stat. He needed to strike while the iron was hot, which was what he was doing. So, Grayson was out in Los Angeles and Samantha was stuck on Nantucket because she wanted to do the responsible thing and give notice to the bakery before quitting.

Now, Javier was freeing her from her obligation to be responsible and professional. So, Samantha was going to fly out to Los Angeles that evening. Grayson had already found an apartment out in LA, and he had already gotten furniture out there as well. All Samantha had to do was pack her personal things, which weren't a lot because Grayson took most of Samantha's things when he moved out to Los Angeles, and fly.

"Okay," Samantha said. "I guess you're just going to have to find somebody else to make the cake for this weekend's wedding. Good luck with that."

Javier just disgustedly waved a hand at her and scowled. "Go," he ordered.

"Going, going," Samantha said.

Then she went home, packed, and booked a flight to Los Angeles.

Grayson was going to be so surprised and thrilled.

The Beachfront Christmas:
Chapter Two

Sarah

Sarah was absolutely giddy. She'd hired somebody to make sure the tasting room was up and running, and the grapes were almost ready to harvest. She had also managed to get a liquor license, so the winery was ready to open. The previous winery owner had already manufactured a great line of wines in the enormous stainless steel tanks in the cellar. So, even though Sarah planned to create wines her way when she harvested the grapes, at the moment, she was going to offer the wine that she had inherited from the previous owner of the winery.

So now it was time to promote the winery. The first thing she did was contact Kayla Brentwood, who was her niece, Samantha's new boss. Kayla was the owner of a very successful bakery there in town, which also had a catering arm that was just as successful. Kayla was quite young, so Sarah didn't quite know why she was such a success. Then she found out that the Sweet Fantasy Bakery originally was started by Kayla's parents who recently died in a car accident, and Kayla took over.

However it was that Kayla got her gig with the bakery was of no concern to Sarah. What mattered was that Kayla was looking for a new venue to hold some of her events, and she was also looking for a new winery to supply her wines. Since Kayla was fairly new to running the business, even though she'd worked for the bakery and catering since she was only 10 years old, she was looking for new blood to partner with. Samantha had phoned Sarah when she found out Kayla was looking for somebody to partner with, and she urged her to contact Kayla immediately.

So, Sarah gave Kayla a call, and the two women agreed to meet for coffee later that day. And then Sarah called Mary, who was her stepdaughter, Julia's, aunt. Mary was watching Julia while Sarah was working. Although Sarah and Quinn had agreed to watch one another's children when they could, as, hopefully, when the winery got going Sarah would be working evenings while Quinn worked days, Sarah would be working day and night until the winery opened officially.

Ava was Sarah's partner in the winery business, and she, too, would be working around the clock until things were ready to go. At the moment, Ava wasn't around because she had an emergency at her home because her pipes had burst for some reason. But she would be coming to the winery later that day.

Mary sounded strange on the phone when Sarah called her. "Sarah," she said. "I'm so glad you called. I think you better get home. Something is blowing up and I need to talk to you about it."

Sarah just scrunched her eyebrows. What was Mary talking about? "What's going on?"

Mary seemed to take a deep breath on the other side of the line. "It's Julia. My sister Hannah has filed a lawsuit."

"What kind of a lawsuit?"

"A custody lawsuit. She wants custody of Julia."

Grab your copy...
vinci-books.com/beachfront-christmas

About the Author

Ainsley Keaton lives with her hubby and two fur-babies in Southern California. When she's not binge-watching *Grace and Frankie, Succession* and *Downton Abbey*, she's reading historical and women's fiction and scouring the beach for sea glass and sand dollars.

www.ingramcontent.com/pod-product-compliance
Lightning Source LLC
Chambersburg PA
CBHW011348010726
47493CB00011B/3010